Praise for *Starlight* and Richard Wagamese

"A cause for celebration. [Wagamese's] work is always spell-binding, comprising powerful stories that get to the heart of Canada—funny, sad, sometimes disturbing and weighty, but always human, no matter the circumstances. When you read a Wagamese novel, there are times you forget that you are reading a book and instead feel as though you have become witness to the lives of his characters. Wagamese was not just one of the finest Indigenous novelists this country has produced, he was one of this country's finest writers, period. . . . [*Starlight* is] a joy to read, with classic Wagamese moments of connections to the land and between characters. . . ."

—*Quill & Quire*

"[A] triumph. . . . This is an important story to know and to experience, from an artist cut down at the height of his powers."

—*Winnipeg Free Press*

"A wonderful and moving story, both tragic and hopeful."

—*Regina Leader-Post*

"What Wagamese does with this novel is set stunning scenes and deliver a moving story about the power of family even if it is an accidental one."

—*Vancouver Sun*

"Richard Wagamese divined the secrets of human scars and knew that broken people are the strangest and most extraordinary people of all."

—Louise Erdrich, *New York Times*

BOOKS BY **RICHARD WAGAMESE**

Fiction
Keeper'n Me
The Terrible Summer
A Quality of Light
Dream Wheels
Ragged Company
The Next Sure Thing
Indian Horse
Him Standing
Medicine Walk
Starlight

Non-Fiction
For Joshua
One Native Life
One Story, One Song
Embers: One Ojibway's Meditations

Poetry
Runaway Dreams

STARLIGHT

AN UNFINISHED NOVEL

RICHARD WAGAMESE

McCLELLAND & STEWART

Library and Archives Canada Cataloguing in Publication data
is available upon request

ISBN: 978-0-7710-7087-7
ebook ISBN: 978-0-7710-7085-3

Book design by Andrew Roberts
Typeset in Sabon by M&S, Toronto
Printed and bound in the USA

McClelland & Stewart,
a division of Penguin Random House Canada Limited,
a Penguin Random House Company
www.penguinrandomhouse.ca

4   5   23   22   21   20

STARLIGHT

PROLOGUE

_____

Nechako Valley, British Columbia

1976

STARLIGHT HELD THE URN IN BOTH HANDS. When he got to the porch he scraped the mud from the heels of his boots on the edge of the top step. Behind him the light was frail. The field was awash in low-lying fog that came with the chill, and the line where the bush began was demarcated by the blurred serrated shadow of tree tops pocking the flank of the ridge. The sun hung in the backdrop of cloud like a yellowed eye. He had to hook the doorknob with a finger to pull the door open and push it back with one shoulder to step through. The house was dim and cool and he took care to step out of the boots, nudging them off with the toe of the opposite foot and cradling the urn to his chest.

He carried the urn to the kitchen table and set it in the middle. It was brass. He held his hands against its sweep and curve. "Fancy for you," he said. "But you were due it."

He went to the fireplace and spent some time with the kindling and birch logs. When the fire took he held his hands out to warm them. A black iron kettle hung from a tripod and he shook it to gauge its depth of water then arranged the tripod legs to hang the kettle over the fire. He sat there staring at the orange burst of flame. Steam curled off the damp of his ill-fitting black suit and he took the jacket off and flung it over his shoulder toward the old rocker set square to the hearth. He tugged his tie loose and yanked the tails of the stiff white shirt free of his pants and sat with his hands dangled over his knees until the kettle began to whistle and he rose and returned with tea bags he dropped in. Then he went back for the urn, a mug, and a handful of candles. When the tea had steeped he used a thin towel hung on a peg to hold the kettle and fill his mug. Then he walked around the room setting candles here and there and lighting them with a wooden match. Satisfied, he returned to the hearth and sat cross-legged on the floor sipping at the tea and watching the dance of light and shadow on the urn. It seemed to shiver like a live thing stirring.

"God," he said. "Never knew how much this place needed you to fill her 'til now."

There was the sting of tears at his eyes and he shook his head to clear them. He'd made it through the funeral without them. Just him, the minister, three local farmers, and a five-woman choir from the church. The old man would have railed at the religiosity, but he'd opted for the ceremony out of a sense of decorum, not knowing for certain what was required or even what was right. But it made him feel in control. As though somehow the one decision gave him a fortitude he lacked. Once the ritual was finished and the farmers eased away like mist across a pasture, he stood in the parking lot, leaning against the wheel well of the pickup. After a time he wandered the town. There wasn't much to it. But he found memories in many of the places and he stood with his hands in his pockets and he felt better somehow in these dim recollections of him and the old man arranging the stuff of their lives in the slow-motion roll of time on those streets. At the school he'd attended it was as though he could hear the voices of the children and see himself running to the truck and the old man waiting with the passenger door flung open, the smell of it and the feel of his work shirt hard at his cheeks when he hugged him. There were scenes like that everywhere it seemed and he took his time working his way around the town. Then, in the late afternoon he returned to the funeral home and sat in the truck and smoked and waited for the urn to be brought out to him. The funeral director, a pasty rail of a man, bowlegged and quick in his movements like a varmint, handed it to him and nodded.

"Thank you for the service," he said. "It was nice."

"It was simple," the man said. "I liked that."

"He'da liked it too."

"Yes. He would have."

He'd driven around with the urn on the seat beside him. He'd thought to drive to all of the places the old man favoured and play the country music station he'd listen to on the porch in the evenings. But those geographies seemed wrong. The music felt out of place. Eventually he'd driven back to the farm in silence and when the light rain fell, he'd stood out in it watching the play of light across the field, the urn slick against his cold, cramped fingers. Now, the fire chased the stiffness from him and he wiped at his eyes and picked the urn up and cradled it and rocked back and forth, singing ragged and rough the one gospel song the old man had known about a home across a river he'd never seen. He let the tears come finally until he'd cried himself out and then stood and walked to his bedroom and changed his clothes. He stoked the fire and blew out the candles and carried the urn in his arms out across the yard to the barn where the horses stood in the stalls, heads draped over the top rails like paintings of ancestors in a great hall watching the procession of the dead. The old man had loved the barn. Sometimes he'd wander out and find him just sitting in it and he'd join him. The two of them would sit silently and eye the ramshackle lean of it, taking in the smell, the low warmth that came off the animals, the way the light as it shifted came to change the barn's angles, the wind making it creak as though there were voices in the beams and joists. When he thought of his life on the farm he would always think of those quiet times in the barn; the old man, neck craned, studying it as though seeing it for the first time every time. It seemed to him then that the old man had wanted to pull it deep into himself and he liked to think he had. So he carried the urn into the tack room and cleared a spot on the shelf where bits and bridles and hackamores hung. He set it there. He stepped back and looked at it, not knowing where else to leave it until he could figure out the proper place to scatter the ashes. This seemed a fine honouring. It seemed the proper place for the old man to rest. He wiped at his face with the flat of his palm. He craned his own neck and studied the barn. There were voices in the beams.

He took his time with the cleaning. He rolled up the carpets in the living room and bedroom and hung them over the clothesline and beat them with a broom. He used the same broom to sweep the ceilings and down the edges of each wall. Then he dusted and waxed every surface before he swept the entire house and flung the dirt and dust off the porch. Then he mopped. While the floors dried he sat in the old man's rocker on the porch and smoked. After a while he rose and washed every dish and pot in the kitchen and set them in the cupboards. There was a box of food he wouldn't get around to cooking that he left on the porch for the Goodwill folks to pick up along with another that held the old man's clothes. There wasn't much. He'd learned frugality and thrift from the old man and they'd only ever had what they needed. There was no surplus. Nothing went unused. Nothing was wasted. The boxes held everything the old man had owned except for the things Starlight had chosen to save. His pipe that he set on its stand beside the kitchen table where he liked it. His rope hackamore, hung on its nail in the mudroom. A pair of boots, shone thin and canted hard at the heels, tucked under the foot of his bed like the old man could rise and step into them. The duster he'd worn when he still rode draped across the saddle set on a tall stool beside the fire.

He walked through the house and made sure everything was in its place and then sat in the old man's rocker by the fire with his legs stretched out in front of him, staring at the hearth. This rough old house, ramshackle barn, the horses, the cattle, and the eighty acres it sat on were all he'd known his twenty years. The only sound was the ticking of the clock on the hearth. It struck eleven a.m. He rose and walked to the front door and opened it and leaned on the jamb, staring out across the pasture with his hat in his hand. He heard a calf bawling and the sound of hoofs kicked against a stall. There was the hard clap of a rifle to the west and then another. Silence. He heard the house beams shift and he turned and looked into it, the feel of it against his face. When he felt tears he turned and stepped out onto the porch, pulling the door closed behind him and locking it. He'd drop the key at the neighbours. They'd leased the land to work as they wanted. They'd tend to the horses and watch over things while he was gone. He had no idea how long that would be. He pushed the back of the old man's porch rocker and watched it move back and forth. When it stopped he strode resolutely to the truck, the crunch of gravel echoing off the barn, and he opened the door and stepped up and stood on the running board with one hand on the roof, eyeing the place before climbing in behind the wheel. He drove out of the yard without looking back. When he got to the road he sat there, the truck idling smoothly and his hands gripping the wheel. There were horses in the field across the road. They were lined nose to tail facing into the light breeze that came from the east. The farm was all the world he'd ever known. It felt empty, alien without the old man. There was a whole other world out there beyond the valley the farm sat in. He pondered that. What he knew of the world beyond the farm was the backcountry, the bush, the rock, the rivers. He knew nothing of cities or books or histories beyond the one he'd made here. He'd been of a mind to leave and see some of that outside world. See himself against the context of it, maybe choose something different for himself in the process. With the thrum of the rebuilt motor shimmying the truck some, the idea of himself against the backdrop of that small farm and the shadow of time passed there hung over all of it, so that when he pulled the truck into a tight U-turn and drove back to the house he felt right and contented in re-inhabiting this world.

BOOK ONE

WILD THINGS

1980

EMMY AND THE GIRL WATCHED THE ROAD. It was full dark. Mosquitoes whined around their faces and they brushed them off, never taking their eyes from the gravel driveway eked out of the purple darkness like a stain. They counted the cars as they turned out and onto the main gravel road to town. Twelve of them. They waited. After a long unbroken silence she motioned for the girl to rise and led her slowly out of the bush. The girl moved well, never snagging or catching a foot on the underbrush, and Emmy admired the stealth learned from the man in the cabin at the end of that driveway. One thing that was good and strong and would serve her well. They stood at the edge of the road. Wary. Alert to any sound or movement that would send them back into the shelter of the trees. There was nothing.

"Reckon he's asleep?" the girl asked.

"You hush," she said.

The girl looked at her wide-eyed, the gleam of them like quicksilver in the murk. She nodded. The man was a deerstalker. He would awake at the push of a faint breath. Except when he was drunk as he would be now but she knew better than to believe in the absolute deadness of drink. She coaxed the girl forward with a fan of her fingers and they crept to the head of the driveway. She stopped and listened. There was nothing and they walked along the edge where the gravel was looser, finer, and where the scrunch of their footfalls would be diminished. Quiet. The burly hump of an owl in a tree. Bats. Mosquitoes and the soft whisper of breeze in the leaves of aspens. Nothing else moved or was heard in that stark quiescence. She found her breath deep in her belly and her mouth opened, each exhalation long and hushed, and the girl was a wraith in the darkness behind her. There was sufficient light for the gravel to be a dim trail wending its way deeper into the maw of bush toward the cabin a half-mile in. They skulked forward.

Eventually the road sprawled open into the yard and she could see the hulks of old cars and trucks and farming equipment the man kept for trade or parts he would sell every now and then. There were ancient implements and bush gear, axes, saws, and pike poles stacked against crates that held turnbuckles or gears or hanks of fatigued rope or hand tools gone weary with rust. It was a sad agglomeration. The air was tainted with the smell of grease and oil and decay. Even the grass seemed to erupt in sporadic twitches like it had to be coaxed outward onto this cheerless flat. The cabin sat beyond it dark as a failed idea, tendrils of smoke from the chimney the only sign of life. The truck was parked at a wild angle with the doors thrown open from when Cadotte and Anderson had lurched out of it, Anderson likely carrying the keg of beer and him toting a crate of vodka, rum, whisky. She signalled the girl to wait and she ducked and waddled to the truck, using it as a screen. The keys were in the ignition as she hoped and she pocketed them in the cheap cotton shift she wore over the work boots laced high on her shins. The girl appeared at her side. She held a finger to her lips and together they crept closer to the porch. They could smell the fire burned down to embers and the scrim of puke and piss and blood that hung on the air.

Cadotte was the man she'd lived with for three years. He was the one she feared the most. He was a brute and he simmered in a palpable silence and stillness that could fill a room with its sweeping malevolence. He was a tall, broad-shouldered man but the sheer bulk of Anderson made him seem tiny in comparison. Anderson existed on the fear his size generated, even in Cadotte. Together they were formidable. They were wild men. The ones they gathered around them were crude and violent, loggerheaded and dim, prone to fist fights and brawls over perceived slights that ended in laughter, hugs, and an indecipherable bond forged by fury and garrulous talk about women, money, vague dreams, and the accrued gossip that passed for knowledge in men who knew only the integrity of their backs and the erudition of fists.

The yard was littered with thrown bottles, cigarette butts, and plastic cups, and as she edged closer to the porch she could hear the thrum of their snoring. She hoped they were thoroughly drunk and would not wake while she and the girl gathered the things they would need to flee Cadotte and the fallow life he kept them in.

The door opened silently. It had been kicked open in a drunken rage months before and Cadotte had replaced the metal hinges with swaths of rubber tire. She stepped into the front room. It took up half the cabin. The woodstove sat in the middle with a couch set along the one wall. It served as the girl's bed. Anderson was sprawled there, face down, with one thick arm hung over the edge, a bottle clutched in his hand. His unruly hair was long and covered his face, half of it stuck to his cheek with sweat. She could smell the fecund air of his breath from across the room. The bedroom was at the back and through the open door she could see Cadotte spread-eagled with his head thrown back against a pillow and his mouth gaping open as he snored all ragged and deep so that the bed creaked with the strength of his exhalations. She motioned the girl to stay put on the porch and made her way surreptitiously about the cabin, scooping up small items and a change of clothing for them both and stashing them in a burlap bag hung from a nail in the wall. She handed the bag out the door to the girl, who took it and headed off to stash it in the box of the truck. Emmy took another sack and stuffed in a heel of bread, carrots, two apples, and some jerked meat. It was all there was. What she wanted most was the money.

The air in the bedroom was ripe with farts and sweat and spat snuff. She took Cadotte's fish basher from its hook on the door jamb and hefted it in her hand. It was heavy and thick and the knurled handle fit into her palm and she felt safer with it. He never used a bank. He always insisted on payment in cash for every small job he did and he carried it in the pocket of his pants in a roll, dispensing it as he thought it was needed for everything that never seemed to include her and the girl. Now he was passed out and she could see the bulge of the roll in the bib of his overalls. She took a deep breath and moved slowly toward the bed. Cadotte never moved. She stepped to the bedside and raised the fish basher high above her head and reached out with her other hand to his chest and held it inches above his overalls. Her fingers grazed the fabric and she felt herself shaking, willing herself to calm but filled with fear like an ache in her gut. Her vision clouded but she gulped and poked two fingers into his pocket and felt the roll of bills. She slid her thumb into the opening and spread her fingers slowly toward the edge of the roll, and when she found it she eased it slowly out of the pocket and lowered the cudgel and stepped back away from the bed.

She tripped on a bottle and crashed back into the wall.

Cadotte groaned and rolled to his side facing her and curled an arm over as though to cradle her and she inched upright against the wall. He opened his eyes.

"Emmy," he slurred. "What the fuck?"

She saw Anderson's hulk fill the doorway out of the corner of her eyes. "S'goin' on, Jeff?" His big arms were raised with his fingers on the upper door jamb.

Cadotte fumbled at his pockets. He swung his feet over the edge of the bed and glared at her. The moon glimmered off the baldness of his pate. He reached a hand up and rubbed at his jaw and stared at the money and the cudgel clutched in her hands. "You robbin' me, bitch?"

"I only aim to take what I need, Jeff," she said, shaking.

"What you need is to put that billy club down and hand over that roll."

"I need it."

"I already said what you need. Do it."

"No."

He laughed. "No? How you figure on gettin' outta here with that cash when all's ya got is that billy against me'n Jumbo there?"

"I'll fight."

"Ain't no use, Emmy," Anderson said. "All's Jeff wants is his roll back."

"I'm leaving, Jeff. Me and Winnie. We're gone."

"You don't leave me, bitch. No one leaves me."

Anderson lowered his arms and stood blocking the door. "Emmy." That's all he said and the rumble of it filled the room and she could feel her insides quake.

"It ain't good, Jeff. It never was. I'm done bein' beat. I'm done hiding from folk on accounta the bruises. I'm just done."

"You ain't gettin' out the door. You think you took a lickin' before? Now you're really takin' one."

He started to rise and she swung the cudgel at his face as hard as she could and she heard the bone break in his nose and there was a warm swath of blood across her. Anderson began to move but then a bottle smashed behind him and he screamed and fell to his knees with his hands reaching for the back of his leg. Winnie stood in the doorway with a broken bottle in one hand. She broke another against the door jamb and stepped forward and thrust it into the back of Anderson's other leg. Cadotte tried to get up but Emmy smashed him in the face again and he fell backwards onto the bed. She heard Anderson moan in a jumble of anger, rage, and suffering and the big man tried to get to his feet but she strode to him and raised the cudgel with both hands and brought it down on the base of his skull. Twice. Three times. He fell to the floor. When he tried to reach for her she kicked him as hard as she could right in the mouth, grateful for the steel toes in her work boots. She could feel his teeth give. There was a gout of blood on her shin. Cadotte was clawing at the sheets trying to get to her but she two-handed him again across the top of the head and he fell flailing to the floor. She kicked him too. Numerous times until she heard the girl call.

"Ma," she said. "Let's go."

She looked at the two men on the floor and there was rage like a keening rising in her throat. She kicked savagely at Cadotte's back and shoulders then moved toward the door and delivered three kicks to Anderson's belly and ribs before the girl pulled at her hand. She gave one final crashing blow to Anderson's head and stumbled across the cabin and lurched out the door onto the porch. The air cleared her head. She stood there gasping, the cudgel falling from her grip and spinning off the boards into the dirt. She heard them groaning in the bedroom. The roll of money was gone. She stared back into the cabin and the girl tugged at her. She had no fight left. They ran to the truck and when it started she pulled away in a wild, gravel-spitting turn, the headlights flooding the cabin, and then she stopped. She stared. Then she got out of the truck and walked back to the cabin. Cadotte and Anderson were stirring. She opened the grate of the woodstove and stirred the embers with the poker and threw in wood until it caught with a lick of flame, the orange light of it making shadows leap behind her. She added more wood until she stoked a good blaze, the snap and crackle of it sending embers jumping out the opened grate. She left it like that. She walked to the truck and got in and closed the door and sat studying the cabin in the mirror.

"Ma?" Winnie said.

"Better odds than he ever give me." She said it quietly, in a murmur, and when she looked at the girl she was crying and she rubbed her cheek and put the truck into gear and headed out the driveway. Behind her the fire spit embers across the parched wooden floor.

2

STARLIGHT SAT BACK ON HIS HEELS and watched them run. In the flush of moonlight they appeared as bursts of shadows between the trees. The lope and bend of them. When they hit the glade the leader dropped into a low prowl, the ears of him flat to the skull and his snout pressed close to the ground. The rest of the pack stayed in the clasp of the trees. The big one swayed his head around then raised his muzzle and sniffed at the air and for a moment fixed his gaze on the man on the rocks then dropped his head like a nod and padded out deeper into the open. The other wolves bled out of the shadow and stood around him. Waiting. In the luminescent blue of the moon Starlight could see the huffed clouds of their breathing. They sat back on their haunches, tongues lolling like dogs, and when they flexed their jaws he could hear the smack of their tongues on canines, sharp and feral, and the piercing whine and whimper of wolf talk. The alpha male sat like a stone, staring intently at the rocks. Starlight felt the hot muscles in his thighs but held his pose, staring back at the humped shadow of the wolf in the glade. He breathed through his mouth. The big wolf raised his head and swivelled it to catch the wind and when he was satisfied he stood, and Starlight was impressed at the size of him. The wolf walked slowly across the front of the rocks and the others trailed behind him, and when he broke to a trot they picked up the pace silently. Starlight waited until the last of them was gone and then slid out of the rocks and began to run behind them.

He ran easily. Like a wolf. He bent closer to the ground and loped, the slide of his feet skimming through the low-lying brush without a sound, and when he found the pace of the pack he angled off through the trees and took a parallel tack to them, keeping them on his right and dodging the pine and spruce easily, his night eyes sharpened by use. He ran with them, the scuttling pace easy after the first three hundred yards.

They broke up the side of a ridge and he could hear the push of their hind feet loosen the talus and he followed the tumble of it up the hard slant. It was a tough climb but he ran it. When he breached the top he saw them gathered in the trees. The big male looked back over his shoulder. Starlight could see the shimmer of his eyes and he felt pinned by the look. He stopped and stood against the open light of the drop. The empty sky behind him. The moonlight. There was nowhere to move so he stood there and breathed and waited and watched the wolf, who kept his eyes on him and opened his mouth and let his tongue droop and huffed his breath so that for a moment it appeared to Starlight as though he laughed, and then he turned his head and studied the trees on the flat. The others sat patiently. None of them looked back. The leader rose slowly and arched and stretched and the others followed suit. Then they broke. In unison. He marvelled at that, the ability to communicate with thought, the language of them hung and shaped on the power of intention, and when they were twenty yards gone he broke into the lope again and followed.

The landscape rolled easily through the coniferous jut and the running was uncompromised by brush. Instead, there were sprinkles of holly and swatches of mountain grass and here and there the plunked forms of fallen trees, decaying trunks he leapt in a single bound while he kept the relaxed prowling pace of the wolves.

He carried nothing but a small pack on his back. He wore no gloves despite the chill and his clothing was loose and warm. His shoes were stitched together out of moose hide and laced tightly. The soles of them were thick pads of felt and he could feel every poke and thrust of the territory he crossed and the tracks he left were mere outlines. The shoes functioned as wrapping for his feet so that the feeling was of being barefoot but protected. They enabled him to run quietly. His hair was short and cropped close to his head, severe like a military cut. There was nothing to catch or snag, even his trouser legs tucked neatly into the tops of his shoes and the sleeves buttoned tight to his wrists. He ran parallel to the wolves and he made no sound.

They angled sharply suddenly and propelled themselves in a hard zigzag up a cut of ridge. It was lightly treed and there were hamper-size rocks and boulders strewn about and he found himself having to clutch and grab at saplings to pull himself upward while he ran. He followed their path. His lungs ached and the muscles at his calves protested and his thighs and buttocks burned at the push but he pressed on. The hard-scrabble face of the cut was inches from his face and he could smell the lichen on the rocks. Dry. Dusty. Metallic almost. He angled his feet to grab more of the face and strained harder

against the gravity he felt upon him like a weight. The wolves
crested the ridge and disappeared. He took deeper breaths and
forced his muscles to work and he could feel the tension in his
neck and shoulders. When he finally stepped quivering onto the
lip of the ridge he was spent and leaned forward with his hands
on the top of his knees and breathed through his mouth and
peered through the top of his eyes to locate the wolves.

They lay on a sloping boulder that poked out over the far
edge. The moon behind them like a giant shining eye. The alpha
male was the only one sitting and he faced the shimmering orb
of the moon with his head slightly raised, like a child wrapped
in wonder. Starlight caught his breath quickly and stood to
his full height. The wolf turned his head. They regarded each
other and the man felt plumbed, known, seen in his entirety,
and there was no fear in him, only calm like the unwavering
gaze of the wolf leader. The wolf stood. He swept his gaze back
and forth across the star-dappled blanket of the heavens and
Starlight followed the look. The universe, deep and eternal,
hung above them: solemn and frank as a prayer.

The wolf sat again and appeared to study the panorama. Then
he raised his snout and yapped a wailing howl at the face of the
moon and the stars thrust out around it. It was high and piercing,
and it brought the others to their haunches and they all stared at
the great silvered orb. Starlight slumped the pack from his back
and took out a camera body and a long lens and screwed them
together quickly. He sidestepped so that he could see the wolves
in profile. They never moved. The dozen of them like acolytes at
a shrine. He knelt and focused on the leader and breathed with
his finger on the shutter. In the frame he held the pocked face
of the moon and the head of the alpha wolf. When the leader

raised his muzzle Starlight pulled the focus tight, and when he opened his muzzle to howl he let him yap the first syllables and then pressed the shutter on a rare and personal moment. The wolves turned at the whir of it. They studied him. He caught them in the viewfinder with the full moon behind them and snapped another. They watched him. Then they turned their attention back to the heavens and began to howl. He felt it in his spine. He felt in his belly. He disassembled the unit and tucked it back into the pack and slung the bag on his back then turned and walked to the lip of the ridge again and stepped down without looking back. The howl of them, ancient, powerful. They followed him back down into the night.

3

THE TRUCK WAS OLD AND BEATEN DOWN by misuse. Still, Emmy drove through the night, grateful that Cadotte had been paid and stayed sober long enough to fill the tank. The girl fell asleep quickly and she sat braced against the door with her legs kicked out along the seat, her chin hung over her clavicle so that she appeared as hollow and destitute as a child of war, which Emmy thought that she was. Life with Cadotte had been brutal. A war of attrition. She pinched her lips together to hold back tears and drove steadily with both hands on top of the wheel, staring at the waving and undulant line of the highway. She had no direction. She had no plan beyond getting them out. Now that she had, it almost seemed that the air was crisper, cleaner than she recalled, and she drank long draughts of it in through the slightly open window. The acts of violence had left her shattered. The face of the old rage she had carried for so long haunted her, the feel of it quaking in her hands and feet frightening her, and she wondered at her ability to escape it, outrun it maybe, like she would have to do if Cadotte survived the fire. His vindictiveness was a scar upon his whole being. If he lived he would search for her, she was sure of that. It would take more than a single tank of gas to put sufficient distance between her and that ruin of a cabin to allow her to feel safe, for herself, for the girl. The only thing she knew for certain was that the rage was her only defence and that she would nurture it, carry it like a sacred ember, fan it, stoke it, keep it hot and ready for the next time, if Cadotte were alive. If he was not, it would still serve her. There were men everywhere in the world.

She'd never had trouble attracting them. She couldn't remember a time in her life when men did not want to touch her, hold her, caress her, and for a time she'd allowed it because it filled the void of loneliness she carried as an orphan and a foster child. Allowed it until it began to hurt. She would not think of those times. She slammed the door firmly shut on that particular quality of darkness. There were monsters there, lurking, skulking, waiting, biding their time before they reached up and took hold of her with cold bones and feral snapping jaws. She'd felt their presence all her life. There'd never been sufficient light to chase them off or if there had been it had only glittered briefly before becoming the shadow she had known and grown used to for a long, long time. It was only the ruthless cruelty of Cadotte that brought the old simmering rage rushing to the surface. It had overwhelmed her. It had cascaded over her like a rogue wave of fear, neglect, abandonment, yearning, emptiness, hunger and want and hate; pure purple, seeping, livid hate for men, for living, for herself, for allowing what she had allowed to happen to herself.

She had chosen Cadotte. That night in the bar in the town she'd only intended to pass through, she'd actually chosen him. The girl had been content being left in the motel with television and a pizza. She was six then. She'd been born in another time when Emmy thought that the tumblers of fate had clicked into a position of permanence. But that man had left as they all had. She looked over at her. She marvelled at the innocence children sink into when they sleep. She wished it would remain in daylight hours but Winnie had never felt peace or anchoring or anything home was supposed to reflect in anything she'd read. At least she wasn't an orphan. Not yet anyway. The irony was that she knew she would die to prevent that from happening. She shook her head at the thought and focused more intently on the road. Cadotte. He was big, strong, agile, charming in a gruff, raffish way, and straightforward with his body, his needs, his wants, his hungers and intentions. She'd let herself flow with that, believing somehow that a man with no secrets around what he was looking for was better than the wheedling, mushy, emotive kind. She'd thought there was honesty in that. She'd been wrong. Almost deathly wrong.

His world was limned by booze. He drank constantly. But she had her own covenant with liquor that seemed to fit with his. The booze allowed the monsters and the darkness to slide away. It allowed her to approach the feel of merriment almost, freedom, and she allowed it into her world as often as the opportunity arose. With Cadotte it rose every day. She was drunk for six weeks. She emerged, pale and shaking, with the girl and Cadotte and an ignoble mess in that calamity of a cabin. It had been a grey day, dismal with sheets of rain and cold so that she shivered as much from that as the drying-out. The girl had stared at her timidly from the corner of the couch and Emmy had held out her arms to her for minutes before she stirred and walked to her and laid her head on her shoulder. She could feel the hot press of a single tear slide down her bare back. Her intention then was to stay until she could find a job and save enough to leave. That had never happened. Cadotte closed every avenue of escape. He imprisoned them by lack. She had been simply too broke to leave.

He took her whenever he wanted, however he wanted. He allowed Anderson and the others to have her at the debauches that happened all too frequently. He beat her. He threatened to beat the girl, to take her too. That was the reason she allowed it—to keep Winnie safe. In the end that was also the reason she fought so grimly to escape. It had been three years.

When she looked over again the girl was awake and staring at her.

"Where are we, Mama?"

"I don't know. Somewhere near 100 Mile House."

"How many miles is there?"

"I don't know."

"I'm hungry."

"Have that apple."

She could hear her biting and chewing and she brushed her hand across her brow to sweep away the tiredness. The fuel tank was less than a quarter full.

"Do you remember how to siphon?"

"Un-huh."

"We're gonna pull over near a farmhouse and I want you to take the gas can in the back and siphon us off some gas."

"All right." She said it dully, disinterestedly, like she'd asked her to take out the trash.

Cadotte had taught her that. He'd taught Winnie to steal chickens, eggs, fruit, vegetables. He taught her to swipe hubcaps, anything metal, and copper wire from cables. Anything that could be turned to cash. Asking her to do this for them caused Emmy a well of shame. She grinned at the girl, more as a means of quelling her sorrow than offering her courage in the theft.

They rounded a curve in the road and she saw the darkened silhouette of a rural place. There was no barn. But there was a truck. She eased to the side of the road and the girl jumped out and she could hear her rustle the jerry can out of the box. She got out of the truck and stood beside her. There was no dog. It would have barked by now. Instead, they could hear crickets in the fields and the whine of mosquitoes around their faces and the soft lowing of cattle. She touched the girl's shoulder and they moved forward together. They walked in the low culvert at the side of the driveway where the grass would soften their footfalls. Nothing moved. When they got to the yard she motioned the girl toward the truck and pointed to herself and then the house. Winnie nodded and scuttled off toward the truck parked a dozen yards from the house. Emmy crept toward the porch that appeared to encircle the building. She could feel her heart hammering in her chest against her shallow breath. Nothing stirred. She slide-stepped to a window and cupped her hands and peered through the glass. When she identified the way to the kitchen she moved along the porch to the back door that led out from it. She waited. When there was still no sound she tried the doorknob. It was locked. She could see the girl trundling the jerry can away from the truck and down the culvert. When she was sure she was away she bunched her skirt up around her fist and punched through one of the small panes of glass. It shattered easily. The sound of breaking glass was muted by the cloth but she could hear the crack of it echo off the shed behind her. She stepped to the side with her back pressed to the wall but there was no sound at all from within the house so she went back to the door and reached her hand through the broken pane and found the doorknob and stepped through into the kitchen. It was large and spacious and the floors were wood. It was a humble kitchen but clean and well tended. The cupboards reached high above the wide varnished counters and there was an old iron stove and a refrigerator of the same vintage. The sink was spacious and enamelled, and there was a pantry just off to the side. She crept to it. The shelves were filled from floor to ceiling and confident now that there was no one home she pulled on the chain she felt against her cheek and smiled.

There were cloth bags hung on a nail beside the door and she filled them quickly with things they could eat on the road. Jams and preserves and cookies and nuts and dried fruit. She took another bag and walked to the refrigerator. She filled the second bag with cheese, milk, carrots, some hard-boiled eggs left on a saucer, and several stalks of celery. On the counter she found a cake pan. She lifted the lid to find a chocolate cake and she dug her fingers into it and ate leaning against the counter. When she saw the girl step onto the porch she waved her in and they both attacked the cake, chasing it with gulps of milk. When they were finished she wiped her hands and face with a dish towel and motioned for the girl to grab one of the bags. She opened a few drawers.

"What're ya doin'?" Winnie whispered.

"We ain't proper thieves," she said in a low voice. "I'm gonna leave a note and say thanks."

She looked at her in an odd way. "Why?"

"They're just like us is why."

She nodded and walked out the door onto the porch with the bag in her hand.

Emmy found the nub of a pencil and a brown paper bag and scribbled a note.

"We're sorry for the damage. We was just hungry is all and all's we took was some food. Sorry."

She thought about signing her name but thought about Cadotte maybe making it here and decided against it. She left the note against the lid of the cake pan. She picked up the remaining bag and walked out onto the porch and put her free hand between the girl's shoulder blades, and they walked casually down the driveway to the truck. The girl put her feet up on the dashboard and she started the truck and eased back out onto the road. She could hear her munching carrots in the dark.

4

STARLIGHT WIPED A HAND ACROSS THE GLASS and the condensation peeled away from the window like the skin of turned fruit. He stared out across the dank yard and he could see them walking through the field toward the barn, the clank of the cow bells dulled by the fog they moved though. They were like wraiths in the faint light. The rain had kept up overnight. When he pulled on his clothes they were still damp. They'd worked late into the evening and he'd been too tired to hang them properly. He dressed slowly. The cold wet of the clothing made him shiver and he clasped his arms about himself and crow-hopped lightly to warm himself. The room was cold and the floorboards slapped icily at his feet. He pulled on his socks and an old wool sweater he kept on a hook on the back of the door for mornings like this. The house was quiet and he stole down the stairs and into the living room.

Roth was sitting on a straight-backed chair in the dark, watching the fire he'd stoked work itself higher, and the soft burn of flame threw everything into shadow behind him. "Colder'n damper than a witch's wazoo out there, Frank."

"Ground'll break easy then," Starlight said.

"We dug that trench all day yesterday. It never broke easy."

"Might now."

Roth eased himself up from the chair and walked into the kitchen and returned with two cups of coffee. "Gotta thank old lady Gramm for makin' up our lunches. But if I get mock chicken again I swear I'll scream."

"Better'n that headcheese we tried last week."

"That there is a fact," Roth said.

"Who the hell ever thoughta eating something like that?"

"Some poor slob in a ditch, I reckon. It's the kinda thoughts that come to a man waist-deep in muck."

"That what you think about?"

Roth laughed. In the dim light he could see the toothless gaps. "Not even. Me, I'm thinkin' of women and good, warm whisky and even better lovin'. What about you?"

He shrugged. He disliked this kind of talk. It didn't lead anywhere and he had no voice for things that held no consequence. "Horses, I guess," he said. "And the smell of the land after a rain like this."

"Yeah, well, you're gonna get a snoot full of the smell of land today. You know they got backhoes for this kinda shit?"

"I always figured a man gets more satisfaction outta workin' with his back."

"Yeah well, you and me got a whole different idea of satisfaction apparently."

"You been with me long enough you oughta know how I work."

"That I do, chum. You also know that they got furnaces that'd heat this place better'n that fireplace, don'tcha?"

"Fire's good for the spirit."

"Warm's better."

"We'd best head out and get them cows milked."

Roth shook his head sadly. "See, the thing with you is, you flat out refuse to look progress in the eye. Not that I don't mind squeezin' a tit now and then, and I do enjoy a cold glass of milk on occasion, but dang it, Frank, how come we gotta milk by hand still?"

"Progress is just a lazy man's word for easy. You get to feel the work this way. Way it was meant to be."

"Is that a fact? Well, why don't you run with them wolves and then sit and paint 'em insteada usin' that camera? Seems to me paintin' and drawin' is how it was meant to be."

Starlight grinned as he raised the cup. He enjoyed this repartee. Eugene Roth had been with him three years and had eclipsed the definition of hired hand long ago. He was a friend now, and a good one, and Starlight couldn't see working the farm without him. "That's a point," he said. "Except I got no hand for art."

"You got an eye for it though. Those are some plumb amazing shots you come back with. How the hell you do that anyhow? Get the critters to pose like that?"

"They don't pose. They just let me see them in their true nature."

"Yeah. But how?"

Starlight sat back in the rocker and let his legs stretch out in front of him. He sipped at the coffee and nodded as the flames broke out in a wide fan of orange and the heat of the blaze pressed against his chest. He reached a hand out to his left and ran it along the edge of the old man's saddle. "The land makes ya equal," he said finally. "Spend time out there alone like I done all my life, it talks to ya, let's ya in on secrets most people never get."

"Good thing I know ya, pal. Folks hear a man talkin' about hearing voices in the wilderness they label that man looney tunes."

"It don't talk in words, Eugene. It talks in feelings."

"See? Now that there'll get ya a standing reservation in a rubber room."

Starlight laughed. "Not as crazy as it sounds. You learn how to listen proper out there is all."

"Maybe I never learned to trust it like you do, Frank. That's why I don't venture out alone on it."

"Maybe ya should sometime."

"I can hunt down a deer and snare a rabbit, sure. But what you do? Disappearin' alone for days or just on a jaunt in the dark? That ain't got a drop of me in it."

"It might."

"Maybe. But what I hanker for sits a lot easier in my mind."

"I know. I know. Warm women, warm whisky, hard country music."

"Now that there is a workin' definition for livin'."

"Well, we work hard enough you might turn that into true."

"Which reminds me," Roth said. "They pay you a lot for them pictures. Why'n't ya just call it a game and do that for a living insteada bustin' your hump the way it was meant to be? Or at least buy a dang milkin' machine! And a friggin' backhoe."

"We best get to it so we can hit that trench."

"Awful anxious for discomfort, ain't ya?" Roth asked.

"Just how I am."

"Never knew no fuckin' keener for muck'n mud before. Sits kinda strange in my whattaya call it? Sensibilities."

"How I was raised."

"Sorry for ya," Roth said.

They rose and walked through the kitchen to the mudroom and pulled on their boots and slickers and then stepped out the door onto the porch and stood watching the rain and eyeing the gauzy hump of mountain through the fog. The trench they'd been digging cross the yard was four feet deep and under a yard across. They'd dug twenty yards of it.

"Coulda backhoed the whole shebang and saved us the slavin'," Roth said. "There's professionals for septic fields and tanks anyhow."

"We're as professional as it gets."

"Ain't no frickin' honour in diggin', Frank. I feel like a gol' damned badger or something."

"Damn good diggers them badgers."

"Varmints is what they are."

"Once we're done the chores we'll get at it. I'll bust up." He looked at Roth. The skinny man just scratched his head. "You follow with the barrow and shovel."

"Leaves me with two jobs. Loadin' and sloggin'."

"Choose then."

Roth rubbed at his jaw. "One's as bad as the other, I guess. You're a mind for it, we'll switch when we get to diggin' out that old tank."

"Sure," he said. "Yell if I'm too fast for ya."

"That'll be the damn day."

He stepped into the wall of earth and swung the pick. It bit into the hard pack and there was a cascade of stones and earth before he yanked the tong back and debris bellied onto the board at his feet with a clatter like shot in a pail. He kicked the dirt back with one foot after each swing. The glint of the pick in the dimness was like the sweep hand of a clock and it drove him to work faster. His muscles loosened. He felt his heat rise and there were beads of sweat at his eyes he cleared with the back of a wrist before plowing the head of the pick deeper into the dirt. He could hear Roth behind him muttering and cursing, the scrape of the shovel on the boards as he loaded the barrow for another trudge to the end of the trench at the house where they would carry it off with a tractor. He made four yards in just over an hour and he was bristling with the effort and the feel of the work in his arms and shoulders.

"Christ, Frank, give it a rest, will ya? I need a friggin' smoke," Roth said.

He set the pick down. They turned the wheelbarrow over on its rim and sat and he twisted a smoke for each of them. The light had grown to a shroud-like grey.

"I remember how hard it was to talk the old man into puttin' in septic in the first place. Used to live with just the outhouse. I come to like the indoor washroom."

"You mean progress?" Roth closed one eye against the rising smoke and stared at him.

Starlight grinned. "Yeah. Okay. Progress."

"Dang. He said the word. Might be there's machines in our future after all."

"I wouldn't bet your wages on it."

"Don't know, pal. You let one bit of progress in, the rest'll come in after it. Why you so deadset against allowin' modern times in anyhow?"

Starlight stood and ground the butt out with the toe of his boot and let the last lungful of smoke trail out of him. Roth stood and they turned the barrow back on its wheels. "Keeping the old place like the old place just sits right in my head. Tradition kinda. Like the old man woulda wanted it kept."

Starlight looked ahead of them at the end of the digging. He could see the slick, bald head of stones clumped into the press of the dirt and he swung the pick and began again. Roth broke into his mutter and they were both soon lost in the mechanical rhythm of the dig.

5

THEY SLEPT IN THE TRUCK. Emmy pulled into a rest area in the middle of the afternoon and they lay their heads back against the door frames and were asleep almost instantly. The patter of rain on the roof woke them. The girl rubbed her eyes with a knuckle and reached for the sack of food at her feet. She rummaged around and found a carrot and gnawed on it and looked at her mother out of the corner of her eye.

"You hungry, Ma?"

"Not yet. I got a powerful thirst, though."

"I could run over to that crick and bring you some water."

"All right. I just need to sit a while."

The girl clambered out of the truck and she watched her cross to the creek that ran along the back of the playground. She seemed so small. Emmy felt a lump grow at her throat and the sting of tears in her eyes and she shook her head to clear them. It wasn't good for Winnie to see her cry. As desperate as things were she needed to show her nothing but strength, endurance, game. She needed to act as though Cadotte were alive and intent on finding her. Winnie. If he found her he'd find Winnie, and when she considered his meanness, his darkness, she felt the hot bile of anger in her belly. She banged the steering wheel with a fist.

"Ma?" Winnie said from outside her door.

She rolled the window down and took the plastic cup the girl offered and drank, and the sleeted relief of the water enlivened her. She got out of the truck and stretched and tousled the girl's hair. The rain was a joyful spray and she raised her face to it and let it hit her square and the girl followed suit. They stood there together. Winnie laughed. She motioned to the truck and they settled themselves and she started it. There was a rumpled road-map in the glovebox and she reached across the girl's lap and got it. She unfolded it and Winnie slid across the seat to look at it too. She pointed to where she thought they were and where they had come from.

"You think we got far enough away?" Winnie asked.

"I don't know. I think we should push on more."

"There doesn't look to be much around here."

"That's what I'm hoping for."

"Whattaya mean?"

"I mean, I think Jeff would think we'd head for a big place. Like Vancouver maybe or Calgary. Someplace someone could get lost in."

"I got lost in the bush once. Remember?"

"I do. And that's where we're headed. Somewhere where there's nothing but miles and miles of land around us."

"Like where?"

"We'll know when we see it."

"I better keep my eyes peeled then."

She smiled. "I guess you better."

She put the truck in gear and they rolled out onto the highway. The gas tank showed half empty. She clenched her teeth and drove while the girl sat up on her knees, staring out the side window at the land flashing by them. According to the map she figured they had enough fuel to reach just beyond Williams Lake. She hoped so. When they ran out she'd have to figure out how to continue. She heaved a deep breath and set her mind to that. Necessity. She would do what necessity asked her to do and she wouldn't allow anything to prevent her from keeping her girl safe. Knowing that, she leaned back in her seat and drove relentlessly.

They drove through Williams Lake. They made another thirty miles and the gas situation became critical. It was early evening and they'd driven past the rain. Now the world was cloaked in grey and she was hungry. The girl had snacked on the food in the sack and Emmy was content to allow her to eat. Now, she felt the need for food herself. But she would resist until she found the resources or the opportunity to get them more. She saw a woman working a horse in a round pen in the front field of a small acreage and she pulled over to the side of the road.

"Stay here," she said. "I'm just going to have a chat with this woman."

She got out of the truck and walked over to the rail fence and leaned on it with one foot on the lowest rail. The woman was doing groundwork with a young horse, leading it with her hand and getting the horse to follow at her shoulder. When she put it through a tight turn she saw Emmy leaned against the fence.

"Can I help you?" she hollered and the horse shimmied but held its place.

"I hope so."

The woman left the horse to stand and walked over to the fence. She was tall and broad with florets of brown hair stuck out of the broad-brimmed hat she wore. Her dungarees were faded and thin and her shirt was flannel and blue checkered.

"Viv Anders," she said and stuck out a hand.

"Emma Strong. Emmy, they call me."

"Well, Emmy, what can I do for you?"

"I'm travelling with my daughter and we've had a touch of bad luck."

"Is that so? What kind of trouble did you find?"

"Someone stole my bag at a truckstop. Took all our money."

"Well, you know, this world is getting crazier and less trustful by the day. That kind of thing doesn't surprise me anymore."

Emmy smiled at the words. "I wondered if you might have a bit of work I could do. I'd be happy to do anything for a meal or even gas to get us on our way."

"Where you headed, Emmy?"

"Vanderhoof," she said, recalling the name off the map. "Thereabouts anyway. I can muck stalls. I used to do farm work when I was a kid. I'm still a good hand with an axe too if you need splittin' done."

Viv laughed. "Well, I don't know how Cliff would take to a woman splitting a cord but I sure don't see the need for you to do that. How old is your girl?"

"Eight, almost nine. Winnie. Winifred. Her name is Winifred."

"Well, why don't you drive up to the house. I'm going to put Cash back in the stall and I'll meet you there. I'm pretty sure I can find something you can do that needs doing."

"Thank you, Viv."

"Well the truth is, Emmy, there's not a lot of folks anymore that are willing to do work for a favour. Reminds me of when

I was a girl and barter was the way of the world. I like to hear that kind of talk. Miss it, really."

She walked back to the horse and Emmy returned to the truck. "We're gonna have to do a bit of work for that woman, but she'll feed us and give us some fuel."

"All right," Winnie said quietly.

She drove up the driveway and parked and waited for the woman to show them what to do.

They forked fresh straw into the eight stalls Viv had for her horses. Then they moved a sack of oats from the mow to the lower level of the barn and then whitewashed rails on three of the partitions where the cattle were kept and finished off by filling water troughs for the stock and the chickens. It was good work and Emmy found herself pleased with it. When they had finished Viv showed them to the gas tank and they filled the truck while the woman went to the house and returned with a box filled with food stuff. Emmy took it and set it on the bench seat of the truck where they could both get at the box while she drove. Winnie doodled circles in the dirt with one foot.

"This really helps, Viv. I thank you."

"You earned it."

"We'll be on our way then."

"A little word of advice, honey, if you don't mind?"

"No. Please. Go ahead."

"Whatever it is you're running from is never really gonna get left behind."

"What makes you think I'm runnin' from somethin'?"

"You don't have a suitcase. No luggage beyond a sack of clothing in the box of that truck. You move like you're afraid you might go sideways and that girl is skitterish as a barn cat."

"I suppose we do look it."

"That you do. Here's what money I can afford to give you. But it's really for that girl. You see she's safe and warm and fed."

"I will. And thank you, Viv."

"Thank me by getting your feet set down somewhere soon. Don't go dragging that child around the country. She needs school and she needs friends. She needs a home. You see to that and it'll be thanks enough."

She handed Emmy a roll of bills that she tucked in the pocket of the shift, then Viv opened her arms wide and swept her into a hug. Emmy stood ungracefully, embarrassed and off-put by the sudden intimacy. When she let her go Emmy raised one hand and brushed awkwardly at a lank of hair. Viv walked around the front of the truck to the passenger side and looked at Winnie, who sat quietly in the seat with the door open.

"You take care, girl. Mind your mother."

"I will," Winnie said.

Emmy climbed behind the wheel and set the roll of bills beside her hip. The women exchanged a long look. She started the truck while Viv closed the passenger door and they rolled down the driveway to the road again. She glanced back the way they had come and wondered if the miles alone would keep them safe. She bit down on her lower lip and quaked briefly, sharply. Then she handed the roll of bills to Winnie.

"Count this," she said and pulled out and aimed the truck northwest, deeper away from Cadotte and the bleak life she'd left behind.

6

THE HEAT WOKE HIM. Then the smoke. Then a panic driven
by rage that allowed Cadotte the strength to crawl away from
the wall and reach a hand up to the foot of the bed and haul
himself to his feet. He heard Anderson moan in the roiling
smoke. He followed the sound to the bedroom door, where
Anderson lay immobile on the floor, one hand reached behind
him, gripping at the seeping wound in his leg.

"Kid," Anderson said. "Never figured on the kid."

Cadotte helped the big man to his feet and Anderson slung
one arm across Cadotte's shoulders and together they lurched
out of the bedroom. The front room was an inferno. But the
flames burned off the heavier smoke and they could see enough
to make their way toward the main door that listed on its
rubber hinges, allowing draughts of air that only fed the flames
higher. Great coughs racked both men. Their eyes burned but
they made the door and together they stumbled out onto the
porch and their momentum carried them forward until they
pitched off the steps and landed heavily in the dirt and twitch
grass. The truck was gone. Cadotte rolled onto his belly and
breathed and eyed the yard. Beside him Anderson groaned
and clutched at Cadotte's knee, so he grabbed Anderson's wrist

and set his heels in the dirt and hauled the man farther away from the house that crackled and spit and hissed and roared with sheets of flame that spewed higher into the night. From far off they heard sirens.

"Bitch," Anderson muttered.

"Gotta get the roll," Cadotte said.

"Ain't she got it?"

"Saw her drop it."

"She's likely burnt already then."

"Ain't knowin' laying out here."

Cadotte stood shakily and craned his neck a few times to clear his head and wiped a large palm across his face. He lumbered to the porch and through the door, and Anderson could hear him hacking. The sirens were closer. Anderson wanted a drink. Cadotte's cursing rose through the yowl of flame. Headlights swept across Anderson and he raised a hand. Fire truck. Ambulance. The sounds of men running, shouting, frantic and alive with urgency. He felt hands on him just as he felt a weightless sliding into darkness. He fought hard against it, clutching his fingers into the dirt, and let his face slump into it, the sandy grit of it rousing him some so that he heard rather than felt Cadotte crash down beside him.

"Found it."

"Crazy fucker."

"Gonna need it," Cadotte said.

It was the last sound Anderson heard before the sheet of darkness fell over him.

7

THEY FINISHED THE TRENCH and dug out the ground around the old septic tank in two days. They replaced the pipes starting at the crawl space under the house and lifted the tank out with a winch on the tractor and set in the new one. It was foul work. But the weather cleared and the last day of work was fair and temperate and they were finished by mid-afternoon, and after showering and shaving and fresh clothes they climbed into the truck and headed for town. Starlight had the developed shots of the wolves in an envelope. He liked to finish his own film. There was a small room on the second floor he'd turned into a dark room, and he'd come to love seeing lives emerge in the fluid washes. He was a frugal man. He'd been raised to know the value of things yet temper it with an understanding of industry and the feeling of one's own work in securing what was necessary and needed. It was a farmer's sense and he bore it proudly. If he was taciturn it was because he found words mostly inaccurate and awkward, and chose economy over the fumbling speeches he endured in other men. Roth was the gregarious one. Starlight enjoyed the rants the skinny man made and allowed himself to take a side in the wild discussions Roth could spark only because he loved seeing Roth's energy fill a room. Now, they sat in silence admiring the landscape; the elongated valley set down between a line of mountains on either side, the farms lush and green with the early summer, and the smell of hay and manure and horses through the open windows. He loved this land. Loved it in a quiet way expressed in a slight crinkling at the corner of his eyes when he looked out across it, and a feeling of calm like silence deep in his gut. He needed nothing more than the farm and the solitary time he spent on the land on horseback or on foot. He knew no word for wild. For Starlight the backcountry was like a prayer or a hymn, and a man approached it the same way: reverently, quietly, fully aware of the awe, wonder, and respect it caused to rise in him. He lived for it and craved it like a favourite meal.

The town was small. There was a single main street with five parallel streets and six avenues slashed across those. The town fathers had chosen height restrictions back when the old man was alive and there wasn't a single building beyond three storeys. The majority of the homes had been built near the turn of the century, with the newer, more modern homes erected along the edges of the town so that entering it was like travelling back-wards in time, and Starlight always found himself slowing below the speed limit as he approached, allowing the atmosphere, at once timeless and rustic, to enter him. It pleased him to come to town. He relished the fact of knowing the people he dealt with, their histories, their families, their faces seemingly hewn from the stuff of the town itself; ruddy and fair and unmarred by things like time and progress. The few times he turned up at church on a Sunday were episodes of great community and he felt proud to be known and recognized. Living elsewhere had never occurred to him again after he'd made the U-turn at the end of his driveway after the old man passed. This was his home and these were his people. He supposed he was old-fashioned. If it were true, he could live with it. His bachelor status was something credited to him rather than gossiped about. Even the fact of his Indianness was just another element in the rich stew that comprised the word *hometown*. He felt no urge to discover more about that. For Starlight the farm was his heritage and culture, the plainspoken earnestness of his neighbours all the language he needed, and the feel of the land beneath his feet all the philosophy and worldview that fed his sense of purpose. A night sky brimmed with stars, the snap and crackle of a fire behind him in the darkness, and the howls of wolves on distant ridges were all the spirituality he'd ever needed. He was not displaced or dispossessed. He was home. In that, he felt keenly alive. Skin colour and difference jangled in his perception of place. He was simply a member of a community like he always had been and he occupied his small place in it with dignity, industry, and an affable neighbourliness he'd become known for. Quiet Frank. That's what they called him. Big Frank too, sometimes, but his size was not his measure. The quality of his stillness was.

"There you go again," Roth said.

"There I go again what?"

"That place you go. You get all quiet and you're plumb gone."

"Sorry, Eugene."

"Ain't no call to be sorry. I'd just kinda like to know where it is you get to."

"Can't say. All's I know is I can see myself doing what I do, hear myself thinkin' what I think, feel myself feelin' what I feel."

"But you ain't there? You're just watchin' yourself?"

"Yeah. That's about as good as I can put it."

"That some kinda Injun thing?"

"Don't think so. If it is I don't know how I come to get it. I expect it's the land."

"You're gonna have to whattaya call it . . . elaborate, pal."

"I don't know. You know how when you're out there miles away from anything, how you can sit or stand in perfect silence and not have to or not even want to move?"

"Yeah. Like last fall when we packhorsed into that lake."

"Like that. Yeah."

"That I can get. So you're sayin' that's where ya go? Into that kinda quiet?"

"Yeah. It just falls over me sometimes. It's what I feel when I'm on the land alone. It's how I get them pictures you like."

"That's gol' darned art that. If that's the reward of it, Frank, I'm all for it."

They eased into the parking lot at the Safeway. Starlight gathered up the envelope with the pictures and the negatives and Roth straightened his shirt and jacket and they got out and stood looking around at the town. It was an amiable afternoon and there were a lot of people moving about.

"I'm headed to Deacon's," Starlight said and raised the envelope. "About an hour, an hour and a half, I figure."

"That's good for me. Got me a date with the barber then off to the Regal for a cold one and a game of pool. I'll meet ya here later," Roth said.

They headed off in their separate directions. Starlight walked easily and gracefully for a big man, like a horse never understanding how large and powerful it really is. But he greeted everyone he met with a nod of the head or a finger to the brim of his hat and stepped aside for the elderly or those of lesser stature or folks with bundles or bags. He wasn't a man to impose himself. Walking was a joy to him. He strode through town casually and was greeted with his name or shouts or waves that he returned in kind. When he reached Telegraph Avenue he turned left down its tree-lined length to the photography studio Elmer Deacon ran out of the main floor of his house. Deacon had been the first person he'd shown his pictures to.

"How'd you come to get these shots, Frank?" he'd asked him then.

"Don't really know. I just know that I grew uncomfortable with shooting animals with a gun except for food and maybe they got my change of energy," he'd said and the idea had felt odd and foreign to him then. It felt more natural now.

"Well, whatever you do, it works. I've never seen such intimate shots."

Deacon had become his agent as his talent had grown. He'd schooled him on the use of the longer lens, the ins and outs of aperture and shutter speed, and how to use natural light so as not to spook the animals. He sent Starlight's portraits out to magazines and galleries and exhibitions. Through the past four years Starlight had shot loons and eagles, bears and mountain lions, wolves and elk and moose, always capturing them in bold, moving attitudes that reflected unseen characteristics. His photographs had become popular and praised and provided him with a good source of income.

The doorbell clanged when he entered and Deacon walked briskly out of the back. "Frank," he said. "Did you get me wolves?"

"I got you wolves."

He handed the envelope over and Deacon laid the prints out on a light table. He bent over closely and scrutinized them.

"Wonderful. Magnificent," he muttered, running his fingers along the edges of the four portraits. He stood up and put both hands on his hips and studied the photographs from a distance. "These will blow up perfectly. McNulty at *Nature* magazine will fall all over himself for these. I think we're looking at a cover. Sure do wish you wrote, Frank."

"Me'n words don't exactly have a workin' relationship on paper."

"I know. I was just expressing a fond desire. If you could capture in words what you've caught in these shots . . . Well, it would be fabulous."

"So you like 'em?"

Deacon laughed. "Like? I flat out love them and so will McNulty. I'll ship them out today, but there's something I want to discuss with you."

"All right."

"I'd really like you to go to Vancouver. There's a big gallery there that wants to mount an exhibition of your work and they'd like you to be there. So would I. It would be incredible exposure for you and your career."

"I'm a farmer. That's my career."

"You're also an artist. An exemplary one. No one, and I mean no one, gets these kind of shots, Frank. They're special. Magical. Captivating. We've done well together, don't you think?"

"Sure. But that's your doin'. I figure a good week is gettin' the new septic in."

Deacon laughed again and patted the big man on the shoulder. "That is a good week. But you could have so much more if you'd let me book you for appearances."

"I appear," Starlight said. "And what I got is what I need."

"I know. Did you ever hear the word *transcend*?"

"Sorry."

"Well, transcend means to lift over, move beyond, rise above. Your work lets people transcend the quality of their lives. Your work literally lifts them up and over and beyond what they believe they recognize. That's the mark of a true artist."

"What does all that mean?"

"It means you're special. Your talent is special. People want to be able to connect with it, connect with you. Hear you speak about it."

Starlight grimaced and scanned the walls of Deacon's studio. Several large prints of his creatures were hung there. He could recall the connections he'd made with each of those animals.

"When I got them wolves," he said slowly, "there weren't no words in my head. There weren't no ideas about how to get 'em. I just ran with them. I don't know how I do that. I don't know why. It's just what I do. I figure if I can ever explain it to someone, I might lose it on accounta it happens without words or ideas."

Deacon nodded. It was a long speech for Starlight, and he recognized the effort it took. "It might become too real," Deacon said. "You might take the mystery out of it."

Starlight looked at him levelly. "Something like that," he said quietly.

He found Roth at the Regal with a pool cue in one hand and a beer in the other. When the skinny man saw him enter he raised the beer in salute and grinned. Roth was one of those young men who seemed to naturally gravitate to his elders rather than finding cronies of his own age. The Regal in the afternoon and the local Legion at nights were where he could always be depended on to be surrounded by loquacious, voluble old men brimming with stories of foreign wars, simpler times, lost virtues, and colourful adventures of misdirected youth. Roth was one of their favourites. He had outrageous stories of his own and delighted in his chance to hold the floor whenever it came. He could swap tales with the best of them, flashing his toothy grin, his hands busy articulating a parallel language in the air, punctuating all of it with a raised glass and a nod or a wink. Starlight figured he was an old soul in a young man's body and he never minded if his friend stayed longer with the elder men than he stated. He wandered over and sat at Roth's table.

"So there I am," Roth was saying. "Higher than the arsehole of an eagle tryin' to make sense of what she was trying to get across to me."

The four old men he was with laughed and eyed Starlight when he sat and grinned at him.

"So as it turns out," Roth continued, "she'd been a stripper once. Nimble little thing. Had more moves than the BC Lions backfield."

"Gotta make some moves ourselves, friend," Starlight said.

Roth looked at him gape-jawed in feigned amazement. "You'd actually deprive these gentlemen out of the end of this particularly arousing tale?"

Starlight grinned. "Afraid so. But there's always another occasion."

"That is a fact," Roth said. "Gentlemen, you'll have to wait for another time for the ending of this adventure. The big guy and I have errands."

They shook hands all around and turned and walked out of the Regal and stood in the late-afternoon sunlight.

"You do know that I was just on the verge of relatin' to those fellas the amazing and mindbending shapes and poses a girl like that can get herself into, don'tcha?"

"Good thing I showed when I did then. You were likely to give heart attacks to those old guys."

"Ruth Ann," Roth said wistfully. "Stage name was Casey Fox. I ever tell ya?"

"You did. I ain't been the same since."

Roth chuckled. "Shame a guy can't hold on to adventures like that."

"I was amazed ya held on when it happened."

Roth roared with laughter and they made their way down the street toward the supermarket.

8

IT SEEMED A SERVICEABLE SIZE. Endako. The town
was a mix of new and old, the newer, bigger, more fashionable
homes in a ring around the outside fringe with the smaller,
more rustic, and history-laden buildings and homes strung out
along the town's centre. Emmy liked it immediately. It sat in a
lush valley seemingly dropped down between the opposing line
of ridges, cliffs, and mountain and the deep thrall of bush. It
was miles away from any larger centre. If there was work here
it would be good and honest. Emmy drove slowly through the
streets and followed the road out of town and into the rural
section to the northwest. She was looking for something in particular. She didn't know where to find it, only hoping against
hope that it actually existed. The girl had rolled her window
down and pushed her face out to let the cool air blow across it.
They followed the grid of concession roads into the bush and
after a few miles she found what she was looking for.

It was a long driveway, rutted and high with grass and weeds,
and sheltered from view from the road by a stand of windbreak
poplars and lilac bushes grown wild along the length of one side.
No one had been there for a very long time. The house was a
squat little building, wooden, with a small verandah in the front.

A shed, busy falling in on itself, sat out behind. The house was greyed with age but the windows appeared whole and while tufts of grass thrust upward through the planks of the verandah there was a chimney and a solid-looking door. An outhouse stood thirty yards opposite the shed. There was a rusted water pump set on the concrete slab top of a well. A laggard wire fence encircled the house and there was a large garden gone to weed and rot to the south side. Paper and various articles of wind-blown junk clung to the walls. She parked the truck on the far side of the house and sat with both hands gripping the wheel, surveying everything.

"This is it," she said.

"We're gonna live here?" Winnie asked.

"Yes. No one will come here. It's abandoned."

"Geez. No wonder."

"It was likely a pretty little place in its day."

"Must not have been if people could just walk away from it."

"All places have stories in them, Winnie. We don't know what this house would say if it could talk."

"It would probably say, 'Ooh, that stinks.'"

Emmy laughed. "Come on. Let's take a look around."

They climbed out of the truck and wandered about the yard. Winnie kicked at clumps of shin-high twitch grass until she found a fallen limb and swept it back and forth in front of her while she walked. Emmy let her gaze travel everywhere. It was sunny and quiet and the breeze felt cool against her skin. She closed her eyes and spun in a lazy circle with her arms flung out wide at her sides and she heard Winnie giggle and the two of them swept around in circles with the ticklish feel of grass on their skin.

"Can we keep it like this if we're gonna live here?" Winnie asked when they stopped spinning.

"Well, we're gonna have to," Emmy said. "For now anyhow. Once I find work and start bringin' in a wage we can save for a regular place. Let's look inside."

They walked to the sad and canted back porch. The boards were rotted out on the steps so they clambered up onto one corner using the support beam for leverage. When she leaned on the door it popped open easily. The air was dry and hot and odoured with dust and how she imagined loneliness must smell. But the walls were kempt except for curls of peeling wallpaper and faded paint, and though the floorboards creaked they were solid. She recognized the careful, accurate work of old tools and the precise, assured feel of callused hands on rough wood, a throwback to dim, younger days she barely recalled and inhabited even less. It was a workingman's house. She admired the wainscotting, the mouldings, and the sculpted corners of door frames and windows. The newel post at the foot of the stairs was covered with dust and she rubbed it away with her palm so she could see the grain of the wood and marvelled at the sheen left upon it by a generation or two of children and elders and relatives in their daily ups-and-downs and tos-and-fros in this house, perched on the edge of a pasture in a valley limned by mountains. This was a house raised from the ground up with a clear-eyed and patient vision. A house built in community. She could feel the energy of its raising and the thrum of the thrust and trajectories of the lives it held within its grasp, nurturing them until they flew away, leaving their calls and shouts and laughter, whispers and talk to be held forever in the wood and beams and walls. There was a part of her she recognized in the old house and a part she did not recognize at all. It left her feeling wistful and she wanted to cry. Instead, she wiped her eyes and walked up the stairs with her daughter trailing along behind.

There were three small bedrooms. One at the top of the stairs to the left and another to the right. Down a narrow hallway a third looked out over the backyard. The windows were guttered by dust and she cleared a circle with her sleeve and peered out across the yard to the adjoining fields then picked her daughter up and let her see too. None of the floors creaked. Winnie went to her hands and knees and peered through the floor grate to the ground floor.

"How come we can see right down, Mama?" she asked.

"This house is old," she said. "There's a big stove down there that they burned wood in and the grates were so the hot air would rise and warm these rooms."

"You could spy on people and they wouldn't even know it."

"You could. But spying was just a little bonus. Let's go back outside and check out the water pump."

Winnie ran ahead of her and Emmy could hear her fling open the front door. She walked slowly out of the house, admiring its quaint, subdued aura of age. When she reached the hand pump Winnie was busy trying to lever it down. She reached past her and laid hold of the handle. It was gritty with rust. It barely moved even when she leaned her weight into it. She had to bounce on her toes to find leverage enough to move it a few inches and then jump up and down a handful of times before the handle dropped to its lowest. She wrestled with raising it again. Finally, after another round of struggle she felt the oxidation give way and the handle was easier to work. She pumped and pumped. She began to sweat with the effort. Winnie watched her with her lips clamped together and a determined look on her face. A small spume of dark brown water spilled from the spout and darkened the steel plate set into the concrete.

"Yay!" Winnie cried.

"Not yet," Emmy said and pumped more furiously. Eventually the brown thinned and disappeared and she coaxed clear water from the well. She cupped a handful and raised it to her face and sniffed at it. There was no hard mineral odour. She took a small sip and smiled. "We have water," she said.

"Yay!" Winnie exclaimed again.

"That's the biggest thing. But we're gonna need some things to clean this house up. I have enough money left for that and for some food. There's no electricity so we're gonna have to only buy what we can eat before it goes bad. I have to find work right away too."

"But we're gonna stay here?"

"We're gonna stay. We're gonna make this work. You and me. We can do this."

"And I get my choice of rooms, right?"

"That's right. But maybe in the beginning we'll sleep together. I'll buy blankets in town."

"Endako. That's where we live now."

"Endako," Emmy said. She looked around the property and along the visible length of the valley. "Who'da ever known."

She bought old-style mops with a rolling bucket that had a press handle for rinsing and a smaller, lighter one for washing walls. She bought several kinds of soap for floors, windows, and walls. She bought a heavy broom. There were blankets on sale at a market and she took four of them and a couple of pillows and a double-sized foam pad to sleep on. With the little cash she had left she bought bread, jam, cookies, fruit, vegetables they could eat raw and a sharp knife to cut cheese and a can opener for the cans of beans, tuna, sardines, and pudding for the girl. The townsfolk smiled at her and took her reticence for shyness and she felt a rural sort of welcome from them and was glad for the brief interactions. Winnie seemed to love the town and ran about ahead of her in the stores, exploring shelves and watching people. Endako was a small wonder to them both and they felt lighter and more keen on creating a home for themselves in the dilapidated house.

She filled the bucket with water from the pump and together they carried and rolled it to the house and up the steps. She bent to the task of washing the floors. It was hard work. The years had left crusts of dirt and dust and she leaned into the washing. It took several trips to the well to clean the main floor. Then she washed the walls. Winnie helped with the reachable parts of the windows, and when she'd finished the walls she cleaned the upper portions and wiped them with newspaper. They worked at the kitchen together. She climbed up on the counters to wash the cupboards and promised herself to get a short ladder as soon as she could afford it. She scoured the sinks and fixtures then rubbed them with a cloth until they gleamed. It took hours, and when the day dropped slowly into gloaming they stood in the middle of the main room and looked around them. The wash was imperfect but it changed the nature of the house. It felt to her like an inhabited thing then, something tended to and nurtured in a way that lends itself to the energy of those who live beneath its beams, and she was happy. Happier in a way she could not recall being before. They went and sat swinging their legs off the edge of the back porch and watched the sun sink behind the purple seam of mountains and the sky come ablaze in sweeping veils of colour.

"Home?" Winnie asked.

"Home," she said.

"For always?"

There were points of light in the swaddle of deepening blue and she looked up at them and the girl followed her lead and they sat there as night came in on its unrelenting tide and the moon came to centre that pelagic expanse. She found herself whispering to the stars, the sky, the pale yellow rondure of the moon, and the small girl sat beside her against that fall.

"If this is how always feels? Then yeah," she murmured. "For always."

9

THEY LOADED THE CHAINSAWS, mauls, heavy crow-
bars, gasoline, oil, chain oil, and sharpeners with a cooler for
their lunches into the back of the truck and headed off in the
first glimmer of morning. There was a stand of dead firs Roth
had spotted during the winter and Starlight had gotten permis-
sion from the rancher to drop and buck them and carry them
out for winter wood. They'd leave half for the owner. Starlight
liked to get his winter wood early. Of all the chores around the
ranch he loved gathering winter fuel most. Late spring and
early summer, when the air was free of heat and humidity, was
the best time, and over time it had become a ritual, a ceremony
he found himself craving at the first seep of melt in the spring.
The old man had worked until his final years as a woodcutter
for extra income and if Starlight stopped to consider it, he'd
probably find connection to him in the act of dropping trees,
in the dry smell of sawn wood, the thin choke of gas and oil and
sweat against the tang of coniferous gum. He could work all day
and barely notice time passing. It was meditation. It was absorbing. It was letting go. Roth, in the three years he'd been with
him, had learned very quickly that the big man preferred to
work in silence and he kept that truce with wordiness until they

broke for water or a rest or a cigarette. Even then he held the reticient ground. He admired his friend and employer for that. The ability to let himself sink into things, to feel them, to understand them through the deliberate actions of his hands and the strength of his back.

So they unloaded the gear and placed it on a ground sheet away from the cutting. They filled the saws with gas and oil and sharpened the teeth of the chains. Then they pulled on the heavy canvas safety pants, goggles and helmets and gloves, drank a few long draughts of water, picked up the saws and mauls and wedge bars, and made their way into the stand of trees. The sun had risen high enough to become like the light of a locomotive through the trees. Birds sang. The snap and crackle of their footsteps through the deadfall echoed in the shadows and they strode purposefully to the farthest edge of the stand. Starlight set his gear down and stood and stared upward, studying the line of trees.

"I figure we work backwards from here," he said. "We drop and limb the first seven. I'll start in to buck 'em while you bring the truck around for loading."

"Seems best," Roth said. "Rough drive over but I done worse."

"You ready?"

"Hell, yeah. I was born ready."

"Drop 'em to the west. Straight out. Yell when you're makin' that last cut."

"Yell what in particular?" Roth asked with a grin.

"Whatever you choose."

"How about the name of the last woman I was with?"

"Geez, by the time you recollect that I'll be smashed to pieces."

"Love's a dangerous business," Roth said.

Starlight shook his head and began walking to the farthest tree in the stand. Roth headed the other way. Soon the air was cut by the cough of cold engines, then sliced open entirely by the whine and climb and attack of open throttles. They set into the work earnestly. Each time either one of them had made their angle cut to direct the fall of a tree, they yelled, and the other stopped and watched while the last cut was made from the opposite side of the trunk and the tree shuddered, then slowly leaned into the cut and eased forward, eventually losing its equilibrium to drop like a sodden drunkard, slamming into the forest floor. They dropped seven like that: Roth walked back to get the truck and Starlight set about removing limbs. It was tough work. He was careful to cut away intrusve smaller branches so he could get at the larger ones. Manoeuvring the saw in those tight spaces was tricky and he didn't notice Roth arrive with the pickup until he paused to rest. He only nodded. The two of them set to limbing the fallen trees.

Now their pace gained in intensity. Once the limbs were sawn, they took to the task of bucking the great lengths of trunk into burnable lengths. The wood was dry and the cutting went quickly. They had to stop now and then to refill the gas and chain oil but they worked until all the trees on the ground were bucked. Then Starlight waved to Roth and they shut down the saws and walked back to where they'd left the cooler and the gear. They found a fallen tree to sit on and Roth took off his goggles and helmet and set them on the ground. Starlight studied him.

Roth was a small man. Slender to the point of attrition but wiry and muscular and a forthright worker. His hands were knobbed and veined, and he was scrupulous about his finger-nails, carving dirt away with a knife in idle moments, trimming them and flicking remnants into the hearth. They were callused and hard, red-looking now with the morning's labour. He rubbed at his head. He'd lost most of his hair except for a tonsure that ringed his pate and faded down to the nape of his neck. His cheeks were sunken from tooth loss and he lacked a devotion to close shaves so that he appeared at first glance to be derelict and slow but he was quick-witted and observant, garrulous and loud, always eager to share ribald, hilarious episodes from a life lived or well imagined. He sat and looked about the glade.

"I ever tell ya much about The Pug?" Roth asked.

"That's what people called your dad."

"Yeah. On accounta he was an aggravating little runt. Small but determined. But the little fucker knew how to work. He loved this job as much as you do, Frank, and I could never get that. I never knew him to hunt or ride horses or fish or anything that'd make him prone to love the cutting. But he plumb loved this. He'd hire on with anyone needed a faller. You know he wasn't trained for nothing?"

"Yeah. I recall it."

"Well, most of the time he wasn't around," Roth said. "He'd get on the trail of a crock of whisky and he'd be gone. Days. Weeks. Fuck, a month once that I remember. But he'd always come back, scratching at the back door like a whipped pup, and my ma would always let him in. He'd be all woebegone and shit, and mope around until his head cleared and the booze fog lifted, and then he'd get right back to work. He'd work anything and he was good at most things that a handyman might do but he never fell into it like he done with cutting. Took me a long time to figure out why."

"What'd you figure?" Starlight asked.

"I figure he always knew he was a shit. Wasn't no surprise to him to be called that, is what I'm saying. And maybe he didn't really know why he was the way he was. He died drunk. I tell ya that?"

"Yeah. You did. First time we talked about my dad."

"Sad. Anyway, what I was meanin' to refer to was how he could be out here and be the happiest I think I ever saw him. Workin' for shit wages but lovin' every minute of this. I thought on that a long time and it was only after he was gone that I finally got it.

"His family life had never been no hell. I never met my grandparents, never knew nothin' about where we come from, who we were, where we started. No one ever become nothing and my dad never did neither. But when he died it started to matter to me that I give him somethin' so he could sit better in my head through the years. I see you out here and it takes me back to what I settled on."

Starlight turned and regarded his friend.

"Now I got no clear way of knowin'," Roth said. "But I chose to believe that my dad knew our roots and he believed we were farmers. And comin' out here, cutting and putting away a winter's worth of wood, was as close to farmer as he could get. He loved it because it made him feel connected, part of something bigger, something he never got the chance to touch. That sound odd to you, Frank?"

Starlight took his time rolling a cigarette. Then he handed it to Roth and while the skinny man lit up he rolled another for himself. He lit up and took a first long drag and exhaled it. "Don't sound odd," he said. "Sometimes we gotta fill in the holes in our history the best we can. I done that too. And now? How's he sit with you?"

"I don't think of him as drunk or a piss-poor provider. I don't think of him as someone who only showed up in my life in pieces. I think of him out here. Smiling. Puppy-dog-eyed, head-over-heels in love with something. If I can give him that, the notion that he loved something, I can give myself the notion that he loved me too. No matter what happened. He sits better with me that way. Funny thing is, so do I."

"You're a damn good man, Eugene."

"Yeah, well do me a favour and tell that to Betty Thoreson."

"You kidding me? Betty Thoreson would about kill you. That's a big strappin' girl."

"Yeah well, life is risk."

Starlight laughed and stood and then they walked back into the work.

They stood in the amber glow of the yard light and studied the wood shed. They'd done twelve trees. They'd bucked and split and stacked and covered half the load with a tarp for the land owner and they'd hauled the rest in the pickup with a walled flatbed trailer on behind. It was late. Close to midnight. The stacking had taken all they had left to give and standing in that mazy yellowed light, staring at a wall of wood stood ground to roof in the shed, silenced them as good, hard work will do to a man left enervated and fuelled in the same measure. Roth nudged him with a fist and Starlight took the tailor-made cigarette held out to him and they lit up and smoked lazily, neither of them ready to surrender the day. They were weathered men. Their clothes were the tough and simple fabric of the farm, the field, the wilderness, and they stood together in that hushed silence, smoking and considering nothing but the gathered evidence of their industry. Above them the congress of stars pinwheeled slowly and a knife slice of moon hung over everything like a random thought. They could hear the sides of cattle shunted against the whitewashed planks of their pens and somewhere far off the skittering soliloquoy of a night bird addressing all of it in plaintive, melancholic notes that rose and fell in counterpoint to their breaths, huffed with smoke. Then they nodded, each to himself, and turned in concert and began the slow, slumped walk to the porch and the house and the rustic simplicity of a bed, a quilt, and dreams wove from the experience of passing through a day, satisfied at the scuffed and worn feel at its edges.

10

THE TRUCK RAN LOW ON FUEL the same day the food ran out. She'd driven back and forth each day determined to find work and found nothing she was suited for or that employers were willing to chance to her. She'd filched garments from clotheslines to augment their wardrobes and to appear more fully rendered for job interviews. There was always a pang of guilt in theft. Still, she assuaged it with the thought that it was a means to a moral end and if that wasn't completely satisfying, all she really needed to do was look at Winnie. It tore the heart right out of her to see the girl gnawing on a swiped tomato as her breakfast. Emmy felt the keen edge of desperation at her gut and a low, simmering anger for Cadotte and every act of acquiesence that had pinned her to the sides of men like him too often and for too long. Now, squatting for refuge in a deserted farmhouse, even that rough circumstance felt better than entrapment, but she still needed to find a resolution, even a temporary one.

She foraged in the cupboard and found a handful of crackers and cheese she scraped free of mould at its edges and placed them on a paper towel that served as a napkin and presented it to the girl along with a small cup of water. Winnie gave her a slip of a smile and ate the meagre food, staring out the window at the break of sun over the fields. The house was chill and damp and she wished for a fire but did not want to chance the smoke. No one had ventured down the driveway since their arrival and she had been careful to avoid any outright signs of occupation. She found herself tired of seclusion and secrecy. Still, she would not relent on the discomfort the lack of a warming fire caused. She turned her mind to a plan for supplies.

In the end it was the stealth and cunning she'd learned from Cadotte that propelled her.

They drove into Endako. Passing the grocery store, she parked on a side street a block away. A gravel alley connected the streets and she left the truck close to its end. Rather than take the short route to the store they walked around the block and she outlined what she wanted the girl to do.

"You need to take people's eyes away from me," she said. "Knock over some stuff and then run like you're in a panic. Fall down or something. While everyone is paying attention to you, I'll slip out with food stuffed in my bag and meet you at the truck."

"How long?" Winnie asked.

"Not long. A minute or so. Just enough so I can get out and away."

"How will I know when?"

"Dawdle around for five minutes. That'll give me time to stash food."

"I'm scared."

"I know, honey. But we have to do this. We have to."

"No one will take me, will they?"

She stopped and knelt down in front of Winnie with her hands resting lightly on the girl's thin shoulders. "No. I wouldn't ask you to do this if there was any danger of that."

"They won't take you away?"

"Not as long as I'm careful."

"Be careful then."

"I will."

They continued their walk around the block and again Emmy was captivated by the casual air of the town and the townsfolk. No one paid them undue attenton but merely nodded or offered a small wave as they passed. Their yards were as well tended as their manners. The parking lot was lightly used at that early hour but there were enough people streaming in and out that she believed there would be enough motion in the aisles to shield her while she did what she needed to do. She got them both shopping carts. When they entered she walked briskly toward the produce and Winnie disappeared into the nearest aisle.

The girl was nervous. For the first while she merely strolled the aisle and then as she turned into the second aisle she began to pick things off the shelves, inspect them, and set them back or lay them in the cart as it suited her. She had no inkling of time passing. Instead, her tight breath seemed to make time slow inexorably and she lost her bearings and wandered loosely along the aisles, wondering how her mother was doing.

Emmy moved purposefully. The bag she carried was wide open and she deftly inserted cheese, sliced meats, fruit, and vegetables. In the cart she lay heavier, bulkier items to give the pretense of shopping. No one seemed to give her a second's notice. Her hunger ate at her but she held it in check and only selected as much as she thought they would need. There was a reluctance in her for this act, as though it tied her to Cadotte, and she wanted it over with as soon as possible. When the bag was full, she ambled along the aisles, waiting for Winnie to create the diversion she needed to flee safely.

By now Winnie was lost in the absence of time. She grew confused over how much of it had elapsed since she'd left her mother. Her hands and skin were clammy, and she felt perspiration at her brow and lower back and it chilled her so that she shivered and rubbed at the length of her arms to warm herself. It didn't help. Her stomach was in turmoil and she desperately wanted to use the washroom but she was spun by internal conflict and roamed the aisles as long as she thought was needed. Then she pushed the cart to a line of registers and stood there, uncertain of what to do next. She pinched her eyes shut. She tried to steel herself to take action but she couldn't find one that seemed loud enough or extreme enough. She quaked.

Then the cashier called to her.

"Come along, sweetie. I'll help you here."

Winnie swallowed hard and pushed the cart to the end of the counter that ran to the till. Her panic was full-on and she had trouble breathing so she began setting things on the conveyor and the cashier smiled at her and began running the items through. There suddenly seemed to be people everywhere. She dropped a can and a big man behind her bent and retrieved it and handed it to her with a grin. She swallowed hard. Now time seemed to swirl and dip and spin and she was disoriented and confused and she reached out to try to haul down a rack of magazines but she didn't have the strength. She tried to fumble down a short shelf of chocolate bars but only two fell out and again the big man behind her picked them up. When he went to hand them to her she broke. She pushed past her cart and ran toward the doors. The cashier called out and Winnie could see her mother staring from across the wide expanse of store. She chose the wrong doors. They were entry doors and she pushed at them with her palms and could see people rushing toward her in the glass and then she turned with her fingers splayed against the glass, twisting one way and then the other, uncertain, terrified and trapped. The white-shirted manager appeared, stepping firmly down the aisle. Her mother walked quickly by, angling toward the exit doors. A man and a woman stepped neatly from each side of the doors as her mother emerged and stopped her in her tracks and a struggle broke out. Grocery items fell to the concrete. Her mother wrestled mightily but they held her and turned her and pushed her back into the store. People had stopped moving where they stood, everyone turned toward the commotion at the front. The manager regarded both situations and then strode toward the ruckus with her mother. Two other white-shirted people moved toward Winnie. She dodged them and ran toward the exit doors. A large arm stopped her. The big man. He knelt in front of her and blocked her flight.

"Easy," he said. "Easy. You're gonna be okay."

She doubted it and began to cry.

There were nine people in the long, narrow room that served as an office. It had large darkened windows and looked out over the store space below, the pasture of it broken into sections by aisles like fences. From here they could see everything and every shopper. The girl stared out over the store and shook her head sadly. Only she and her mother were seated. The rest milled about or inched for space in the cramped quarters: two store managers, the cashier, two security people, a policeman, and the big man. Everyone seemed tense or aggravated or both. Except for the big man. He leaned against the back wall and arched an eyebrow at Winnie when he caught her eye and smiled.

"So, Miss Strong," the policeman said. "This is your daughter."

"Winifred. Yes," Emmy said.

"Your intention was to not pay for anything," the officer said. It wasn't a question. "If I read this right she was supposed to act as your diversion."

Emmy pressed her lips together and nodded. She stared at the floor, clenching and unclenching her fists. "Yes," she said.

"You know it makes you both guilty?"

"Yes."

"You also know that asking a child to participate in a crime is a crime itself?"

"Yes."

"Then why?"

"We're hungry."

The officer shook his head. He looked at the store manager and they were both silent. "Putting up a fight at the doors wasn't a very good choice either," the policeman said. He spoke directly but kindly.

"No. I know."

"It doesn't leave me much room here, Miss Strong. When people are hungry they can get a voucher from one of the churches or their welfare worker. No one has to steal in this town."

"I'm not on welfare."

"Seems to me if you're hungry with a young daughter then maybe you should be. Where do you currently reside?"

Emmy looked at him. "Nowhere."

"Nowhere? Everyone lives somewhere, Miss Strong. We don't have a homeless issue in Endako. Are you just travelling through?"

"Yes," she said.

"But we got a home, Mama. You said." Winnie looked at her imploringly.

Emmy squeezed her eyes shut and wiped at their corners with a knuckle. "It's not a real home, Winnie," she said quietly.

"Are you staying with friends? Camping somewhere?" the officer asked.

"We got a house," Winnie said.

"Where is this house if you don't live anywhere, Miss Strong?"

"Out of town a ways. North and east. It's abandoned."

"Two-storey place? Kind of grey clapboard siding. Well with a concrete slab cover out back with a shed?" the big man asked but didn't look at her.

"Yes. That sounds like it."

The big man looked at the policeman. "Sounds like the old Wilton place, Jensen. Been derelict since I was a teenager. Surprised it's still standing."

"So you're squatting there, Miss Strong? Is that what you're saying?" Officer Jensen asked.

"I never thought no one would mind," she said. "We cleaned it. We're taking good care of it. We're not botherin' anyone."

"I'm going to have to call Child Services," Officer Jensen said. The store personnel nodded grimly.

"What does that mean?" Emmy asked.

"Well, it means a couple things. I'm going to have to charge you with shoplifting and contributing to the delinquency of a minor. Without a fixed address, you're not going to be released and someone has to take care of your daughter. Child Services will put her somewhere. She'll be taken care of while you're away."

"Where are you going, Mama?" Winnie asked. She was crying. She stood up and walked to her mother, who reached out and drew her to her chest and cradled her there, staring up at Officer Jensen, wild-eyed and fearful.

"I have to pay for the groceries," Emmy whispered.

"How long is that gonna take?"

"I don't know. These people will take care of you while I'm gone."

Winnie grabbed tighter hold of her mother and buried her head in Emmy's chest. "No," she said. "No, Mama. No."

"I was caught, Winnie. I was caught. There's nothing I can do."

Winnie turned to Officer Jensen and looked up at him with a stricken face. "Please, mister cop. Please don't do this to us."

Jensen removed his cap and ran his fingers through his hair and glanced around at the others like he wanted to be rescued. "I'm sorry," was all he said.

The big man stood up and stepped closer to Emmy and Winnie. "Why are you squatting in a fall-down old building?" he asked quietly.

Emmy gazed up at him. The size of him rattled her. Her features shook with the effort of speaking. "We're out of money," she said haltingly. "And food. I been trying to find work but there's nothing out there for me. I figured once I got work I could save for a real place."

"Where's your home?" he asked.

"Don't rightly have one."

"Ever?"

"It's a long story, mister."

"Frank," he said.

"It's a long story, Frank," Emmy said.

"Man run off?"

"More like we done."

"Drunk?"

"That's part of it." She looked at him openly. "Like I said. It's a long story."

Starlight stared at her for a moment. Then he turned, strode to Jensen, and whispered to him.

"Mel, you wanna come out with me'n Frank?" Jensen said. "The rest of you can wait with Miss Strong and Winifred here."

The store personnel nodded while Frank, Jensen, and the store manager walked out and shut the door behind them. They could see them talking on the small landing above the stairs. Frank spoke at length and then the other two took their turns. Then Frank and Jensen spoke to each other before concurring with the manger, opening the door, and stepping back into the narrow room.

Jensen walked over and sat on the edge of the manager's desk facing Emmy.

"Miss Strong, Mister Starlight here is willing to pay for the groceries you tried to steal. Management has agreed to that so there won't be a shoplifting charge. If there's no charge on that, I can't rightly charge you with the other offence. It was wrong, make no mistake about that. Clearly wrong, and you put your daughter at risk. So I could reasonably ask Child Services to look into this, and you would still lose your daughter for a time until this all got cleared up. I need you to understand that."

"I understand," Emmy said.

"But you can't go on squatting either. Without adequate and safe housing, Child Services would apprehend your daughter until such time as you could secure a job and hold it until the court was satisfied you were stable and had stable housing."

Her voice shook. "I understand that too."

"Most importantly, I need you to realize that this was a desperate act that had the potential to separate you and your child. It was foolhardy and dangerous. Simply making charges go away does not clear you from responsibility in this. Now or ever. Do you hear me?"

"I hear you."

"Good. I really hope you do because we're going to go out on a limb here and try to help you and your daughter. You need shelter, you need food, you need gainful employment. If those were made available to you, would you take them?"

Emmy stared at him, surprised. "Of course. Yes. Sure. I mean, yeah."

"Okay. Frank, or Mr. Starlight, is in need of a housekeeper. He has room in his farmhouse for you and your daughter. There are two of them there. Mr. Starlight and Mr. Roth. You'd be responsible for laundry and cooking and housekeeping. It's not forever. It's just to help you get your feet under you and provide for your girl. I'll speak to Child Services and they will make an appointment for you with a caseworker who will inspect your living conditions at the farm and ensure that Winifred gets into school right away. You and Mr. Starlight will be held to their conditions and rules. Do you have any questions?" Jensen asked.

"Yes," Emmy said. "I do." She looked at Frank, who put his head down under her gaze. "Why are you doing this?"

The big man squinted in concentration. He looked at Jensen, who regarded him kindly. He pressed his hands into the pockets of his jeans and then pulled them out and clasped his fingers together, then unclasped them, and dropped his hands to his sides.

"For the girl," he said finally.

He studied Emmy.

"And because I guess I'm drawn to wild things."

THE MEN STOOD IN THE HARD SUNLIGHT and stared back at the hospital. They'd reset Cadotte's nose, stitched up his face, and shaved his head to suture the gashes and he swore as he began to unravel the wrappings. Anderson had stitches over his head and face and was standing on crutches. His hamstrings had been cut deeply and walking was difficult with the staples they'd used to close the long, ragged punctures. Both men were gaunt from days in their beds and thirsty and eager for drink. They smoked and regarded each other.

"What's the plan, Jeff?" Anderson asked.

"Don't rightly have one. Figured on sitting with it over a jug or two."

"But we're gonna find her."

"Damn straight we're gonna find her. I owe that bitch some pain. And she toasted my digs."

"Can't get far. That tank wasn't full."

"Full enough. I imagine they got far enough to rest up. Emmy'd figure something to keep them moving." Cadotte threw the butt of the cigarette onto the pavement and ground it out with the toe of his work boot. "Way I see it, she'd go where it's easier to hide. Calgary. Vancouver. Bigger place."

"Make it harder to find her."

"S'what she figures. Me? She's dumb as a sack of hammers. She'd leave a trail anywhere she goes. And she's got the kid. Makes it harder to move without bringin' attention on herself."

Anderson scowled. "Sounds right. Thing is to choose."

"Me, I'd say Calgary. She got a thing for twang and two-step and tall, lanky cowpoke fuckers," Cadotte offered.

"Seems as right a place to start as any."

"We gotta take your wheels. You got any loot stashed?"

"I got a roll buried in the yard. You?"

"Just what I fetched from the fire," Cadotte said.

"That was some crazy shit."

"Had to be done. Soon as I come to, I knew I wasn't lettin' her skate on this."

"Still. You're lucky to not have roasted your ass," Anderson said.

"Close enough for rock 'n' roll anyway, pal. We're fixin' to be gone a long while. Way I figure, there's a lotta work in Calgary, Edmonton, wherever. We can keep ourselves goin' while we track the cow."

"Whatta I got keepin' me anywhere?"

"Same. All's I got now is this hate on."

"Me too," Anderson said. "The kid's okay. I don't hurt no kid. But Emmy's got some hurt comin', that's just a plain fact."

"We were like to be killed," Cadotte said. "She left us to die. She lit that cabin up on purpose. Takes a cold and heartless fuck to do that. I figure to see she gets the same. Only final. No let-up. No mercy. This ain't no hunt-me-down-and-slap-me trip. You good with that?"

"I wouldn't let a man do that to me. So I sure ain't gonna let no woman."

"Good," Cadotte said. "I got nothin' left in the tank for Emmy. Fact is I coulda chucked her and the kid a long time ago. I was just hangin' in for the tail."

"That was some good tail. Drunk or not," Anderson said. "Gotta give her that."

Cadotte caught Anderson's eye and grinned. "Maybe we take a last taste of that before we off the bitch."

Anderson smiled. "Yeah. Make a day of it. I can dig it."

Cadotte nodded. A cab swung into the parking lot and he raised a hand and flagged it over. They climbed in and as the car turned out of the parking lot and aimed for Anderson's place both men sat straight, immobile and silent, staring ahead of themselves out the windshield. There was a grim, dark air in the car. The driver flicked his eyes nervously in the rear-view mirror but something in the set of the big men behind him kept his gaze firmly fixed on the road.

12

"SO LET ME GET THIS STRAIGHT," Roth said. "You go into town for butter and eggs and come back with a woman and a young girl?"

"That's the short of it," Starlight said.

"Well, that sets it then," Roth said. "I can't ever let you go into town on your own again."

"They needed help."

"We ain't exactly the whatcha' call dinner at six, fetch my slippers sort."

"Don't gotta be."

"How you reckon?"

"Way I see it, she cleans, washes, fixes meals and lunches for a while. The girl starts into school how she should. We live the way we live. When they save enough money to move out on their own they move and nothin' changes."

"'Ceptin' I gotta be all charmin' all the time."

Starlight grinned. "Best behaviour is a good thing sometimes."

"Well, shit, Frank. I don't ever rightly recall bein' on best behaviour. What ya see is mostly what yer gonna get from me."

"It's just until they get their feet set under 'em."

"Says you. Me? I might kinda get used to bein' treated like the squire of the manor."

"You can't even pick up your smelly socks."

"I suffer from a lack of lessons."

"What ya suffer from is kindly bones."

"I got plenty of kindness in me. I'm just worried how this is gonna affect our lifestyle."

"Lifestyle? You call this a lifestyle?"

Roth pursed his lips and scanned the room. "She's grim but yeah," he said. "This is mouldy bachelor chic. Takes a studied hand to create this ambiance."

Starlight shook his head and smiled. "You and your words. I swear you're better educated than you let on."

"Part of my charm," Roth said. "Woo the women with the rollin' lilt of language."

"Well, there won't be no wooin' going on while they're here. This is straight-up work for her, a home for the kid, and some regular eats for us. That's all."

"I hear that. I can do that. But lordy, I can't be held responsible for the effect of my animal magnetism on womenfolk."

"You just try to keep it under wraps," Starlight said. "We oughta sort this place out some before they get here."

"You're a kind-hearted bugger, Frank."

Starlight studied Roth gravely. "I know how it feels," he said quietly.

"How what feels, bud?"

"How not havin' a place feels. I ever tell ya how I almost left here?"

"No," Roth said.

"Was after the old man died. Place was hollow. Didn't feel like there was nothin' left for me here. So I leased out the land to my neighbours, got them to look out for the house, and was gonna head for somewhere to do something for some reason. I never did sort it out in my head."

"But you're still here," Roth said.

"Yeah. I am. But I actually got to the end of the driveway. Sat there looking east, then west, wonderin' what the hell was callin' me. It was home. Home was callin' me. I thought behind me was as empty as the road in front of me. It was sad, that feeling. Deeply sad. Sadder'n losin' the old man. I come to know right there that when you figure ya got nothin', goin' back and movin' on can feel like it's all the same direction."

They sat in a deep well of quiet. The house creaked in the push of summer wind. A horse whinnied. Roth stared at the floor and then slowly raised his head to look over at his friend, who sat straight in his chair with his hands cupped in his lap. Roth splayed his legs out in front of him and the scrape of his boots on the wood made Starlight glance over and the pair of them eyed each other in the dim shadow of late afternoon.

"Awful glad you stayed, Frank. I got me a belly full of that feeling too before I got here."

"Home," Starlight said. "Comes to be a truth you carry in your bones. Figure if I can help someone find that, I'm doin' a good thing."

"Best thing, I figure," Roth said. "Count me in, pal. We know anything about this woman?"

"She's got a wildness in her, that's a fact. But she's strong. You can feel that. And she surely loves that little girl. Other than that, I don't know. But I think a person could do worse than having a streak of wild runnin' alongside strength and love."

"Amen to that," Roth said.

They arrived in a dark green Jeep with the Ministry of Child and Family Services crest emblazoned on the doors. Jensen pulled in behind them in the old and battered pickup Emmy had parked close to the store. Emmy and Winnie climbed out slowly, peering at the fields, the outbuildings, and the house. The girl looked in amazement at the horses grazing in the pasture. When she caught Starlight's eye he grinned and she brightened. Jensen strode over to stand beside the social worker, a young, willowy woman with clear green eyes, good posture, and an earnest, open expression. She introduced herself as Madelaine Orr.

"Maddie," she said, shaking hands with Starlight and Roth.

The pair of them had dressed for the occasion. Roth's face gleamed a scrubbed and ruddy pink and he had his ring of hair patted down with gel. He'd clipped his fingernails but hadn't quite erased the brownish yellow tattoo of tobacco at the edges of his thumb and forefinger. He rubbed his hands along the thighs of crisp new dungarees. Starlight wore new black jeans. His hair was cropped short and he'd shaved the line of his sideburns plumb and straight. His hands had been worried at with soap and a brush and looked raw and brown and were held closed at his sides like a pair of rocks at the ends of his sleeves. Both of them wore work shirts with metal snap buttons they'd done up to the neck and fastened closed around their wrists. They each wore stout cowboy boots polished to a high sheen.

Town boots that had never seen the inside of a barn or the dust of a field. They stood straight and nervous in the canted light of late afternoon, blinking and casting their eyes about, uncertain of where to look.

Maddie introduced Emmy and Winnie to Roth, and the skinny man swallowed hard and nodded as he shook hands with the woman and flared his eyes wide at the girl, not knowing what to say. He tucked his hands in his belt and swayed a little. Starlight looked at Jensen as if waiting for directions.

"Well," Maddie said brightly. "We should go inside and show Emmy and Winnie around. Maybe later you can show them the barn and the animals. You'd like that, wouldn't you, Winnie?"

"I like the horses," Winnie said. "And I heard chickens. I like chickens too."

Starlight and Roth flicked glances back and forth. Neither of them said a word.

"Let's go have a look then," Maddie said, and the two bachelors startled and hustled to the porch to open the door and then stood like sentries waiting for the others to follow. Maddie and Jensen grinned. When everyone had entered, the two men followed and stood side by side in the kitchen, watching the woman and the girl investigate the old house.

Starlight noticed what he'd always failed to notice. The kitchen was cramped with the juts and pokes and peninsulas of their living. Pots rinsed but unwashed piled on the corner of the counter. Candles gone to stubs in hardened pools at the centre of the table with its rough and scarred wooden top that could have used a wash and oil. Along the edges of the cupboard doors were thin lines of black from field-hardened fingers easing them open, and a thin filament smeared a pair of drinking glasses clumped down and abandoned beside the enamelled canyon of the sink. The curtains lank and haggard at the windows. Chairs akimbo around the table. Seed catalogues and equipment brochures strewn on unused seats. A pair of sturdy coffee mugs, grim with stains at the handles and the inner lips, set beside an ashtray heaped with butts and dead matches. He watched Emmy to gauge her reaction.

She scanned the room with pursed lips and nodded. She looked at Maddie but didn't speak and then wandered slowly through the darkened rectangle of the doorway into the living room. Roth regarded Starlight with arched eyebrows. Everyone followed Emmy and Winnie deeper into the house.

The house faced due east and in the late afternoon it was dim. The bachelors had neglected to leave a light on and Roth fumbled with the switch on a pole lamp that threw everything into focus. The room was another bramble of living. There was no proper bookcase so there were photography magazines devoted to wildlife and coffee table books piled beside the chair that Starlight favoured and Roth's was marked by strewn copies of tabloids and word search puzzles. A threadbare carpet covered most of the space in front of the hearth, blackened by years of neglect, and the windows were dressed by floor-length draperies that deepened the press of shadow and dark. Sweaters and small hand tools and bits of cord and a hacksaw blade sat on the counter of a hutch beside an old-fashioned radio. The glassed shelf space held nothing but unused candles and several dead watches.

"Cleaned it as best we could," Starlight said and coughed into his hand.

"Mmm-hmm," Emmy said and moved slowly about the large room lifting things and running her hand along surfaces.

"Eugene's got the downstairs room there," he said. "I have the room on the left at the top of the stairs. There's a big bedroom that looks out over the yard at the end of the hall that'll be for you. Bathroom's up there too."

She stared at him wordlessly then turned and made her way up the stairs with Winnie trailing after her. Maddie followed them and the three men stood together watching them leave. They eyed one another.

"Whattaya figure?" Roth asked neither of them in particular.

"Coulda done better with the cleanup," Starlight said.

"Thought we done a good job," Roth said.

"Not for a lady."

"Or a kid neither?"

"Can't know."

They could hear them moving along the hallway upstairs and opening the door to the big room at the front of the house.

"It's a fine old house, Frank," Jensen said. "They don't build them like this anymore."

"Was a bachelor house when the old man lived here. Still is now. Never figured on no women," Starlight said.

"It's a good thing you're doing. You know that, right? The squat they were in wasn't fit for anyone."

"Seemed right is all."

The two women and the girl came back down the stairs. Emmy looked around the living room again and then stared at Starlight and Roth for a moment. "How do I wash clothes?" she asked.

"Old lady down the road takes it in for us," Roth said.

"I do my own wash."

"Sink then," Starlight said. "It's how I always done. There's a line out across the yard."

"You'll need a washing machine if there's to be four of us."

Roth straightened and glanced at Starlight. The big man swept his gaze around the room. "Well, we dug in that new septic for somethin'," he said.

"If I'm to cook proper I'll need a bigger fridge. And a small freezer."

"Ma'am?"

"If you want me to housekeep I'll need to be able to house-keep proper," she said. "I can make a list of what I'll need. We need a television for Winnie for one thing. Can't expect her to sit around in silence reading equipment catalogues every night."

Jensen grinned and put a hand to his face to cover it. Maddie just studied the bachelors with good humour. The pair of them shuffled their feet and appeared ready to bolt.

Roth stuck his hands in his pockets then pulled one out and rubbed at his jaw and regarded Starlight with a grin. "Progress," he said.

Starlight nodded. "So the place is fine for you?"

"It needs a lot of work. Men don't know a whit about taking care of a place. But it's sturdy and warm. Could use more light. Can we chuck them curtains?"

Starlight looked shocked. "They been here forever."

"I think I can tell."

Jensen coughed into his hand. Maddie pressed her lips together and her eyes glittered.

"Ah. Yeah. Sure," Starlight said.

"Growin' things," Emmy said. "A house needs growin' things in it and this place has none. Be surprised at how much it changes how things feel."

"Always felt pretty good to me," Roth said.

"You're a man."

Roth shrugged. "Yeah."

"Men can feel good in a cave or a lean-to."

Starlight looked at Jensen, who shook his head in merriment.

"So you'll stay? You'll take the work?" Starlight asked.

"What about school? How will she get there?"

"Bus picks up kids along this line regular every morning," Roth said.

"I don't do no extras. You get what you get. You want extra, you do it yourself."

"Sure," Starlight said.

"And I don't pick up after nobody. You put dishes in the sink and clothes in a hamper. That'll be on the list by the way."

"Anything else?"

"A helping hand now and then is a good thing."

"Okay."

"But most important?" She looked at the two of them. Roth rocked on his heels and Starlight glanced at his shoes. "Most important is thanks. Thanks for bringing us here. Thanks for helping me get things in order for my girl. We won't be no bother to you."

"You ain't asked what I owe," Starlight said.

"It's me that owes," she said. "Wages? Hell, that'd be gravy."

———

She made a supper of chicken, roasted potates, and corn. Starlight and Roth cleared the magazines from the chairs and they sat at the old wooden table eating wordlessly. The girl set down her fork every now and then and stared at the adults, and when she made eye contact with either Starlight or Roth the men would look down at their plates or stare off at a corner of the ceiling. Her mother ate slowly. Jensen and Maddie had departed, and the four of them had negotiated their way around the house under a canopy of silence that had only dropped lower and closer about them so that the meal was heavy with discomfort. Every scrape and clink only accentuated it. The men finished first and sat square in their chairs, waiting for Emmy and Winnie to finish. When she finally set down her fork, Emmy coughed lightly and rose and began to gather plates and cups and set them in the sink. She ran hot water to fill it and added soap and stood there watching the suds spread with her back to the men, who looked back and forth at each other in silence before finally standing and setting their chairs deliberately against the table. They gazed down at the girl. She twirled a lock of hair and waited for them to speak but neither of them knew what to say so they moved around the end of the table and made their way to the door leading to the mudroom and the back porch.

"Chores," Roth said.

"Thank you," Starlight said to Emmy as he passed.

She nodded and began to stir the soap around a plate with a beat-up sponge she had found under the sink. They closed the door behind them and she could hear the clunk and gather of them preparing for the barn.

Later, when they returned, the house was quiet. The lamps were left on and a fire had been laid in the hearth. They sat in their chairs and smoked and watched the flames, listening for any sound of motion from above. They heard nothing. Eventually they reached for their reading materials and smoked and read until one of them yawned and stretched and stood and the other followed suit. Roth walked into the kitchen to shut the lights and to flick on the yard light. Starlight glanced about the living room and set things straighter and neater where they'd sat and then stood quietly until Roth emerged from the kitchen.

"Reckon they'll be warm enough tonight?" Roth asked.

"She's a chill old house."

"Girl might get cold."

"Wouldn't want that."

Roth led the way to his room and they opened the closet that held his few articles of clothing and a shelf piled with blankets and quilts and extra sheets. Starlight reached up and hauled down a pair of wool blankets. He held one to his face and sniffed at it. "Dust," he said. "And age."

"We ain't used other'n what's on our beds as long as I recollect," Roth said.

"Gotta be somethin' up there won't smell of time."

They spent the next few minutes sniffing at everything until they settled on a pair of quilts. They were rag quilts. Each panel different from the rest and sewn carefully. They felt warm and comfortable and the men took them in the crooks of their arms.

"How'd these come to be here?" Roth asked.

"Christmases. Sometimes the ladies on the line would bring things over for the old man. These were some of those offerings."

"When's the last time a woman been in this house, Frank?"

13

THE FIRE HAD BEEN BANKED IN THE HEARTH when he came down the stairs in the purple world of morning. The house was warm. Roth sat smoking in his chair in front of the fire and shrugged to him as he passed. Emmy was stirring oatmeal and there was the smell of coffee. She brushed a loose strand of hair back from her face and he watched the straight back of her and the firm set of her shoulders.

"Good morning," he said.

"There's coffee on the stove. I don't know what you take in it so there's sugar and milk on the table." She didn't turn around.

"Black," he said. "Same for Eugene."

"Well, Eugene is going to have to serve himself. Same as you."

"Ma'am," Starlight said. He poured them each a cup and toted them into the living room and shrugged at Roth as he sat. They lifted the cups to their lips and sipped and Roth grimaced.

"That's some brew," he said.

"Strong is sure," Starlight said.

Emmy stepped into the doorway wiping her hands on her skirt. "There's porridge ready."

"We don't usually eat before chores," Roth said. "Coffee and a smoke is all. Most times just the smoke."

"Well, you'll eat now," she said. "I'll fix a proper breakfast when you're done. We'll need to shop today."

"We done it last week," Starlight said.

"Well, what you done isn't gonna allow me to feed you proper. I'm going to need a lot more."

"We ain't the biggest eaters," Roth said.

"And look at ya. You're a bean pole."

"I like to call it lean. Like a panther, you know?"

She shook her head sadly. "Damn hard-put-upon panther you ask me. We need things. Pure and simple."

"All right," Starlight said. "We can get some things from your list too, if you got it ready."

"It will be."

The men rose and followed her into the kitchen. There was a small stack of fresh toast and jam set out on a plate and a pair of steaming bowls of porridge. They sat awkwardly, unused to the ceremony of eating. Roth sipped at his coffee while Starlight slathered jam on a slice of toast. Slowly. Taking his time. When he looked up she was eyeing the pair of them coolly.

"I swear it's like the two of you never done breakfast."

"Oh, we done it," Roth said. "But more like hanging our faces over the sink, jawin' about work that needs doin'."

"This is different, that's sure," Starlight said.

"Well, you brung me here to do a job and a job is what I mean to do. If I have to teach you to eat proper, that's part of my job. I aim to make you feel right about your choice."

"You done good so far. This is fine." Starlight lifted a spoon of the porridge in salute.

"It's porridge. Take a heap of doin' to mess that up."

"Still and all, I thank you."

"Me too," Roth said. He crammed a whole slice of toast into his mouth and sat back and chewed roughly then chased it down with a big slug of coffee. He grinned at both of them.

"Gonna take a whole lot of teachin' for some. I can see that already," Emmy said. There was a light in her eyes and Starlight felt glad to see it.

"You slept good?" he asked.

"Yeah," she said. "I did. Thank you for the quilts. Can't believe I never heard you. Musta been more tired than I knew. Turns out we only needed the one."

"The girl? She sleep okay too?"

"She still is. Sleeping in a truck is no way to rest. And a bundle of blankets on a wood floor don't lend itself to good sleep neither."

"I'm sorry that had to happen to you."

"Better'n what it was."

She looked at the floor and the two men fell into silence. Neither of them wanted to break her quiet. They ate keeping an eye on her and saw her tremble slightly then gather herself with a long indrawn breath and raise her head to look at them.

"But I won't bother you with that," she said. "Now finish off that slop and get them chores done. I'll have you a real breakfast in a couple hours. I seen an old triangle on the porch. I'll bang that when it's ready."

"That'll be good," Starlight said. "We got a thin day. The three of us can head into town once we eat."

"What's that leave me to do?" Roth asked.

"You can ride that fenceline and see if we need to pull wire again."

"Sounds like fun."

"Prowl it," Starlight said. "You know. Like a panther."

Emmy smirked. Roth grinned and drained his coffee and followed Starlight into the mudroom.

They drove the first part of the way into town in silence. Winnie sat between Starlight and Emmy and leaned forward on the edge of the seat with her hands on the windshield, staring at the country they drove through and pointing out various things to her mother. Emmy sat with one leg crossed over the other and one arm slung along the window frame of her door, nodding to her daughter and rubbing her back in small circles. Starlight gripped the wheel with both hands and struggled for words. None were forthcoming. He drove easily and leisurely so the girl could see more. The silence was a living thing between them. Emmy jostled in her seat to partially face him and he peered at her out of the corner of his eye.

"Can I ask you something?" she said.

"Sure."

"Can I get some money up front? I need to get Winnie some school clothes. She hasn't any. Maddie said she'd give us a day or so to get sorted before she takes us to register her for school. But I thought since we're going to town . . ."

Starlight nodded. "Yeah. Yeah. Sure. I can see to that."

"Thank you, Frank."

"You're welcome, Emma."

"Emmy."

He glanced at her. "Thank you, Emmy," he said.

"It's always Frank? No Frankie?"

"No. No Frankie. Just Frank. Franklin, really."

"You don't strike me as a Franklin."

"How do I strike you?"

"Like a Frank, I guess."

"What I am."

The silence descended over them again. Winnie sat back and leaned on her mother. Emmy draped an arm over her shoulders. Frank pursed his lips and drove but finally got the gumption to look at Emmy directly.

"The way you done our feedin'," he said, "was like you know how farmers eat. Somethin' small then chores then a bigger breakfast later. How come was that?"

"A long time ago," Emmy said slowly, "I was a farm girl. My family had a farm. I don't remember lots of it. It was a long time ago."

"You ain't that old."

"It ain't the years. It's how you feel in them."

He studied her briefly then concentrated on the road. "Yeah, this kinda life stays with ya. I tried to leave once. Couldn't."

"Where did you have a mind to go?"

"Don't know. Couldn't figure it. But I couldn't reckon not bein' here either once I got to the road. So I turned around and stayed. It ain't lots. But it's mine and I don't owe nothin' on it."

"Lots do, I suppose."

"Yeah. My neighbours struggle. She's a hard go. I was lucky."

"That's been in short supply for me."

"Luck?"

"Yeah."

"I'm of a mind ya make yer own."

"Easy for you to say. You got it."

"I suppose that's true. Take things for granted me sometimes."

"It's nice you can afford to."

He drummed his fingers on the wheel. He'd never been much on conversation and when they dead-ended he was always at a loss over the silence he found himself wrapped in. Now, with her, he felt awkward as a kid. He didn't know how to talk to women. His world had been a world of men and he was used to their gruff, clipped talk and liked it since it matched his own inherent reticence. He admired those men like Roth who could roll out conversation like a favourite old carpet and stand on it and hold forth for long stretches at a time. Talk had always been a struggle for him. He found himself more fully in wombs of silence than in the hard light of the world of talk.

"Sorry if that sounded bitter," she said.

He shook his head. "No matter. If it was I missed it. Me, I don't figure anyone's story is free of grit. Mine ain't."

"That's a good word. *Grit*."

"Kinda wraps it up. Don't it?"

"Some," she said.

It had always seemed to Starlight that words had edges to them. Not so much like endings or finalities but more like where they stopped. There was an edge there like the lip of a cliff where words came to teeter, the brink of their flow sudden, exhilarating in the shock of the drop at their feet, so that everything was out of balance for an instant. It seemed to him that the choice of the next one determined poise or plummet, though he couldn't lend words to that idea. Instead, he'd always just felt it. His taciturn nature was built on the grounding act of silence until he could parse the next right thing to say. Right then, he couldn't, so he allowed the talk to dwindle and they drove on in silence.

When they entered Endako he slowed and let them see it. The girl knelt in her mother's lap and leaned out the open window. People on the sidewalk waved to him and he raised a hand cordially or nodded. Winnie waved excitedly. Emmy sat stolidly staring straight ahead. He could see questions on his neighbours' faces. When he parked on the main street and began walking, Emmy and Winnie trailed behind him, and he greeted people as he passed.

"They know you good here," Emmy said.

"Been here all my life."

"Must feel good."

"I don't know any other way of feelin'."

She nodded grimly and matched his tempo. They walked side by side with Winnie holding her hand. As they passed, Emmy could see people squint in confusion and when they tried to meet her eyes she lowered her head and tugged the girl along.

"Don't know exactly what you're looking for, but all the shops are on these few blocks so let me know when you see somewhere you'd like to look," Starlight said.

"Right there seems fine," Emmy said and pointed at a small clothing store.

"I'll just go to the bank. I'll be outside when you're through and ready to cash out."

He strolled off. Townsfolk were everywhere, drawn by the mild weather and sunlight, and he walked easily to the bank and stood in line waiting for the tellers and eyeing people in their busyness and scurry. He was drawn to people. He found them fascinating. They were as idiosyncratic as creatures in the wild and he admired them for the sprouts of wildness they showed when they weren't doing the expected or the proper thing. He mused that if he were a better talker he might even have wanted to photograph them the same way he did the animals.

A tall whip of a man in a Stetson, roper boots, and a faded denim shirt with his dress pants strung by suspenders turned to address him. "See you took in that shoplifter and the child, hey, Frank?"

"Took in a woman and a child that needed help is all."

"Seems to some of us that that might come across as peculiar for you. You and Roth. Couple bachelors under the same roof as a woman who don't give off much in the way of proper."

"Well, you know, Chapman," Starlight said slowly. "There's two things that you and your friends know about me without question."

"And what're those?"

"Well, you know that I'll help anyone anywhere needs a hand if I can do it at all. That's one. The second is that I don't brook disrespectful talk from no one about anything." He canted his head and raised an eyebrow and looked at the man earnestly.

Chapman blanched. "No disrespect intended, Frank. Apologize if it seemed that way. It's just that, well, you know. It's a small town. Stuff gets around."

"Ain't no stuff to get around."

"It's just that you bein' Indian and all and her bein' white . . ."

Starlight shook his head sadly but never broke eye contact with Chapman. "Me bein' whatever I am never raised no concerns with nobody about nothin' all my life. Never expected it to start now."

"I'm not saying anything specific, Frank."

"Then why say anything at all then?"

"People talk is all."

"You're people. Whatta you say, Earl?"

Chapman glanced quickly over his shoulder toward the tellers. There were still three people in front of him. He turned and looked at Starlight, agitated and nervous as a fence-caught steer. He huffed out his cheeks and shuffled his feet and stuffed his hands in his pants pockets. He glanced over Starlight's shoulder and out the door to the street. "I guess I'm saying be careful, Frank. This kinda thing? Well, it's not done around here. People get nervous."

"I been the same me year in year out."

"I know. I'm sorry I said anything."

"Good you done, Earl. Good I know how some folks are feelin'. Some folks. Not all. You hear?"

Chapman stared at him soberly. "I hear."

A teller summoned Chapman and he turned and walked to the counter and leaned on it with his forearms. Starlight felt a hand on his elbow and he turned. There was a prim-looking lady in a brown skirt and natty ruffled white blouse peering at him over the top of her glasses.

"Main Street," she said. "You can always depend on something worth recounting later, can't you, Frank?"

He grinned. "Sure can, Mrs. Gaines."

"Don't you worry about anything. This town is better off having a proper young man like you being a part of the community. I for one applaud what you're doing, and if you or that woman or girl should ever need anything, you know where I am." She smiled at him.

"Emma," Starlight said. "And the girl is Winnie."

He heard his name called and he turned to take his place at the counter.

"You make sure to give Emma and Winnie my best then. And Chester's too," Mrs. Gaines said.

"I'll do that," he said over his shoulder. "And tell Chester I got room to graze twenty head if he needs the range."

"I'll let him know. Take care, Frank."

Emmy was just finishing up at the store when Starlight walked through the door. He held out an envelope to her and she took it and held it in both hands in front of her waist and gazed up at him. She was tall but she had to raise her head to look squarely at him. She felt at a loss for words so she peered into the envelope.

"This is too much," she said.

"Thought you could use a few fresh things too," he said.

She put a hand to her mouth. He could see her blinking and felt embarrassed and glanced about the shop.

"I could," she said finally. "I'll just pick out a few things."

"Take your time," he said.

She nodded. Neither of them moved. He put his hands in his pockets and rocked on the balls of his feet but that made him even more uncomfortable so he reached out and fingered a man's shirt while Emmy slipped away. He ambled around and found the girl holding up a sweater and pirouetting in front of a mirror. She saw him in the glass, lowered the sweater, and looked at him worriedly.

"Sorry," she said.

"For what?" he asked quietly and sat in a chair beside the fitting room door.

"You're buying us this 'cause we can't get things for ourselves. Ma says I'm s'posed to be gracious."

"You just enjoy it is all."

"What is *gracious* anyhow?"

He splayed his hands. She came and stood in front of him, the sweater draped along the floor, so he reached out and picked it up and hung it across her shoulders. She smiled.

"Me'n words like that don't often collide," he said. "Eugene is the word man. But if I was to guess I'd say it meant we're supposed to be all serious and grim."

"How does that look?"

He put his face into a stern-looking grimace and stared at the floor. Winnie laughed.

"I don't think I could do that without laughing," she said.

Starlight grinned. "Me neither to tell ya the truth. But I think gracious is all about acting like you'd kinda wanna do the same for someone else."

"I would," Winnie said. "Really. I would."

"Then I think ya got gracious nailed."

She went back to her slow spins in front of the mirror. Emmy strode up to him with her arms full of clothing. Her face was flushed. "What you give me will take forever to pay back," she said. "But I used it all."

"Ya earn it out is all," he said. "You don't owe."

"We ain't had new things in a long, long time. We're used to used. Or the Goodwill. Sometimes the clothesline discount too I'm ashamed to say."

He regarded her kindly. "Sometimes ya gotta do what ya gotta do."

"You done that?"

"Me? No. But I ain't had much use for lots of things. Few simple ordinary clothes and such always felt most right to me. How I learned, I suppose."

"Seems a good way. Still and all, it's good to have some things back of what you got on."

"Good for the girl."

"Yes. I thank you most for that."

"What it's all about. You go on ahead and cash out and I'll wait outside and help you tote it to the truck."

Emmy turned and waved at Winnie, who joined her at the till and looked over her shoulder and waved at Starlight. He raised a hand awkwardly and held it there until she turned away. He stepped out of the store and sat on a wooden bench to the side of the door. People moved passed him and he nodded to those he knew. He thought about a cigarette but there was no ash can nearby so he held his makings in his hand and leaned forward with his forearms on his thighs and studied the traffic moving by. He hadn't liked the exchange with Chapman. It bothered him but he had no words to organize his thoughts around it so he sat and let his guts settle and when he felt at ease he stood and stretched and leaned against the wall to wait. Emmy and Winnie emerged a few minutes later. He reached out and took three bags from her and left her with a smaller one to carry in each hand. They walked slowly to the street with Winnie skipping ahead of them and he made sure to make eye contact with everyone passing by. He lifted the bags into the box of the old truck and prepared to walk to the grocery store across the block and down another.

"You just going to leave this here all in the open?" Emmy asked.

"It's a good town. No one's gonna bother your stuff."

"You sure about that?"

"As sure as I am about anything."

"Not the kind of place I'm used to."

"It's easy to find your footing here. Just walk. You'll see."

"They must think I'm not much of a person."

"Way I reckon, it's how you regard yourself that counts. What I seen? You got no reason to look down in front of nobody."

She stopped and faced him. "You don't know me."

"True," he said. "I don't. But like I said, I guess I'm drawn to wild things."

"I know. I wondered about that. What did you mean exactly?"

He pursed his lips and stared at the sky. She watched him consider the question and when he looked at her it was earnestly and she waited for his words to form.

"I can't rightly say exactly," he said finally. "But I kinda think I could show you."

They walked into Deacon's and the buzzer announced their arrival. Deacon was on the phone and while he looked surprised to see him he waved at Starlight and then bent back to his conversation. The three of them wandered about the studio. Winnie was captivated by the photographs. She stood gape-mouthed and stared at them and when Starlight led them past the office and into the anteroom where his work hung she ran ahead and stood in a pool of light and gazed raptly around at the images. Emmy roamed from print to print. She squinted hard at the creatures captured by the lens and rendered so magically within the frames and glass. Starlight stood and waited while they took in all of the prints.

"These are unbelieveable," Emmy said. "The same photographer took all these shots."

"Yeah. Same guy."

"It's like you can see them breathe. I can see why you like them. I like them too. Love them, really."

"Do you think I could have one of these for our room?" Winnie asked.

Deacon entered the room with a flourish. "Well, little girl, I'm sure Frank would be happy to let you hang one of his prints in your room. I'm Deacon. This is my studio."

He held out a hand to Emmy, who took it wonderingly and eyed Starlight as he looked at the floor. Then Deacon knelt on one knee and held out a hand to Winnie. She took it with surprise and stared at Deacon, who smiled and reached out and ruffled her hair.

"Emma Strong and her daughter, Winnie," Starlight said.

"Emmy," she said.

"Well, I'm mighty proud to meet you, Emmy. You too, Winnie. I see you have an eye for good pictures."

"It's like going to the zoo," Winnie said.

Deacon laughed. "Yes. Yes, I suppose it is. Frank is a real magician when it comes to getting close to creatures."

Emmy looked at him, startled. "These are yours? You took these?"

Starlight merely nodded.

"Frank is a marvel," Deacon said. "His photos are becoming famous. I'm proud to be his agent. We're becoming quite a team actually."

"How? How do you get these kind of shots? I never seen anything like this," Emmy said.

Starlight glanced around the room. Then he walked around and examined several of the images and the three of them stood where he had left them, watching his silent appraisal. When he turned and faced them the bowl of light he stood in rendered him darker, harder, with the gaunt expression of an ancient warrior, and when he raised his head to look at them there was an obsidian glimmer in his eyes and they stood mesmerized, waiting for the words to fall.

"Wild things," he said. "Always kinda felt wrong to me to say that of them. They ain't wild. Not how most people come to mean anyhow. You watch 'em. See how they are with each other. They're tamer'n us. I think on accounta they know how to love outright and us we gotta learn how to do that. I see that in 'em. How they're tamed by love. Not just each other. By the land. The mystery of it. The pull of the moon. The sky. The feel of it all. That's what draws me. That big open in them. It's what I try to feel when I'm with them. What I try to see and shoot, if I'm lucky. That realness."

He walked across the room and stood facing Emmy.

"You say I don't know you. Might be I see more of you than you do. With your girl. That outright love. Me, I figure that's worth saving."

He walked out of the room and they stood there watching him leave. None of them prone to words.

14

CADOTTE STOOD LEANING ON THE RAILING of the fire escape behind their hotel room, staring away across the city. The jut and angle of it. There was a low stink of gasoline and smoke and garbage just below the fresh air of morning. He scowled at it. He could taste it at the back of his throat. The slick grime of it. He hated cities. There was no order here. The jumble of things confounded him and he wanted the security of open space, the rambunctious wild where things behaved the way they were intended to and even the sky could be read if you took the time to learn its language. But these were strange thoughts for him. He blamed it on the hangover and wanted a slosh from the crock laid under his bed. He took the time to light a cigarette and ran his eye the length of the avenue to where the garbage trucks lumbered along with their amber lights blinking and wondered if they would find her here. Wondered where she might have chosen to hide. Wondered if she could feel him hunkered down and prowling. Wondered if that keen edge of fear tickled at her belly and made her nights long and daunting. He hoped so. He wanted that for her. He wanted her to feel the crush of his vengence approaching, relentless as a thunderclap. He ran a hand along the puckered ridges of scar at the back of his head. Bitch.

He still got dizzy, found it hard to concentrate in those periods between the addle of drink, like now, leaning on a rusted fire escape behind a rat-trap room over an alley desperate with discarded syringes, condoms, clothing, trash, busted televisions, and the splayed forms of drunks and street kids and the mugged and lost and broken who would rise soon to take their places in the grim lines into places where they ate and shat and cadged relief in whatever shoddy form it was offered. He had no time for these desperate losers. It was only her that brought him here. Another score to settle when he found her. He'd find her. He was certain of that. This was only Calgary. This was only the beginning of his search. When he lent his head to it he could see the two of them stalking her the way they'd flush deer. Slowly, patiently, bleeding into the background unobserved and stealthy, knife blades honed and ready for the quick, deliberate slash of the throat that would bleed it out quickly, the sticky tack of it on his palms and fingers and the coppery, dusty taste of it on his lips. He wanted that. It was what drove him. That and the feel of the fire on his skin. It wouldn't leave him. Those scorched and sere places where no hair would grow and even blood seemed wont to avoid so that he rubbed at them throughout the day and the dry rustle against his palm rendered him rageful again at the nearness of a death he hadn't invoked on his own.

He heard Anderson groan through the open window. He crushed out the cigarette and flung it it into the alley. Today they'd start their hunt.

He opened the door and walked between their beds and sat then reached under for the bottle and raised it, unscrewed the top, and guzzled. He wiped his mouth with the back of his hand. Anderson lay on his side eyeing him. He looked back at him and held out the bottle. Anderson rolled onto his back and hiked backwards on the bed and leaned on the headboard and reached for the bottle and drank. He set the crock between his legs.

"So what's the plan, Jeff?"

"Much as I got, not much," Cadotte said.

"That's encouraging."

"Hell, it's a big town. So I figure we take it area by area. She ain't got much so she'll be trolling for some mark to take her home. Could be she already found him. They'll be around. We just find the bootleggers, the rubby-dub joints or the low-end country bars and Bob's your uncle, there she is."

"That easy?" Anderson asked.

"She's gonna leave a trail wider'n a drunken moose."

"Figure?"

"Hell, yeah. She only knows what she knows. Only goes where she goes. Chooses what she does. Not exactly no rocket scientist."

"Suppose not. Still, gotta be a wrinkle or two we ain't thought of."

Cadotte took the bottle and held a slosh in his mouth and nodded. "Could be. But I doubt it. She never shown me no gumption to wrinkle nothin' but bed sheets."

"Might be she's diff'rent. Likely knows we'd be trackin' her."

"She don't even know for sure we're breathin'. Far as she figures you and me got ate up by that fire."

"Wonder why she never set it to burning right?"

"She did do. That friggin' cabin would go up like dried tinder. She knew that. And that knotty pine'd be throwin' embers right off the hop. She knew that too."

"Wonder if she was givin' us a chance?"

Cadotte flopped back onto the bed and let his boots dangle off the end. He took another drink and held the bottle out to Anderson without looking at him. "That's soft talk. She figured the fire boys would find the grate on the stove wide open and believe we was drunk and fell asleep with it that way. Caused it our own selves. Only smart move she made. Gets her offa suspicion."

"Exceptin' for the knife wounds and the thumpin'."

"Told ya. We'd be figured drunk and disorderly. Fightin' each other."

"That's a lot to figure when you're scared shit."

"Takin' up with her, Anderson?"

"Fuck no. I'm still tryin' to scope out if there's wrinkles we ain't thought of. Tryin' to see how much thinkin' she done. Like maybe we'd be so grateful we didn't roast we'd let her skate."

"Skate nothin'. She's gettin' what she's gettin'."

"And the kid?"

Cadotte put his hands behind his head and stared at the ceiling. Anderson drank and watched him think. He set the bottle on the floor and the thunk of it echoed dully off the bare walls. Cadotte swung his legs off the bed and sat up, fixing Anderson with a hard, blank stare.

"No breaks. No mercy. It's a one-hole job," he said.

BOOK TWO

———————

DEER STALKER

THEY WERE WHITEWASHING THE FENCE around the main yard. It was a warm morning and they'd both stripped off to their undershirts. Roth dangled a smoke from his lips and drew on it while he worked. Starlight moved intently and the slap of the wide brush on the wide planks left no splatter on the grass at his feet. They were quick and efficient and the job had been going well since the dew had burned off. They heard the scrunch of gravel and the ping of small stones against the undercarriage and the wheels of the vehicle before it turned slowly into the expanse of the yard. They kept working.

"Morning, Frank. Eugene."

"Morning, Maddie." Starlight hadn't even looked up.

"How'd you know it was me?" she asked.

"Car sounds different than a truck. Truck'll throw more echo offa the barn."

"Coulda been any car."

"Coulda," he said. "Wasn't."

"Truth is we don't get much traffic, Maddie," Roth said. "Process of elimination ain't a tough call out here."

"Well, you two are a constant source of surprise for me."

"Farmers is all," Roth said. "Get good ears after a time. Nose and eyes too."

She smiled. They stood in front of her like a pair of kids waiting direction. They looked so innocent, so eager with their scrubbed and shaved faces they obviously took pains to effect with Emmy and Winnie around. They leaned forward a little, staring at her with eyebrows arched. She almost laughed.

"I need to talk to you about something, Frank. It's about Winnie."

"You want me to step away?" Roth asked.

"No. You're part of this. You should hear everything. If that's all right with you anyhow, Maddie," Starlight said.

"That's fine," she said. "You're right. Eugene should hear this too."

"Eugene," Roth muttered. "Ain't no proper name for a man. Mule maybe. Good hunting dog or a sheep."

They laughed and Starlight led them over to wooden chairs set under a tree. They sat and the men leaned forward, eyeing her.

"Winnie's having some trouble getting along at school," Maddie said.

"She ain't quick enough on the uptake?" Roth asked. "Seems a smart enough thing around here."

"It's not that. She can do the work and she does. It's just that she seems to have trouble getting along with the other kids. Particularly the boys. She fights them. She's been in two altercations already. This last time she gave Miles Paterson a bloody nose."

"Snot-nosed little bugger, that Miles," Roth said. "Always figured him for a schoolyard sissy. Fightin' girls ain't no real boy thing."

"Eugene," Starlight said quietly. "What do you figure the trouble is, Maddie?"

"It goes beyond the whole new kid in the room thing, Frank. She just seems to have a bad attitude toward boys. They tease her, make fun sometimes like boys will do and she retaliates. It's not good."

"You spoke to Emmy?"

"I will. But I wanted to run something by you first."

"And that is?"

"Well, it's kinda coming out of left field here, and you can tell me if it's too odd a thing to ask or too much even."

"Just go ahead and ask, Maddie," Starlight said.

"I have one of your pictures hanging in my living room. The one you took of the heron in the fog? It's where I got the idea. I thought, that picture holds so much peace in it, so much serenity, such a pervasive calm. I wondered if being out on the land might help her. I wondered if you could spend time with her out there and show her what you find there, that connection to something bigger, maybe she might respond to that."

"Respond how?" Starlight asked.

"I'm hoping with the same kind of calm," Maddie said. "It worries me. Neither of them speak of where they came from. But I know that they were running. No one makes the kind of choices Emmy was making out of assurance. She was scared. So was Winnie. They're still scared."

"They are kinda like a pair of barn cats them two," Roth said. "Skittish. Take flight and cover easy."

"That's why I'm worried for Winnie," Maddie said. "I'm thinking it has something to do with men."

"If you thought that then why figure this was the place for them," Starlight asked.

"Well, you two aren't really men."

They glanced at each other and then turned their gaze to her.

"We ain't?" Roth asked.

Maddie grinned. "I'm sorry. That came out wrong. What I meant was you two aren't typical men. You're rough and gruff, Eugene, but you're tame and gentle when it comes down to it. And, Frank, you've never been anything less than polite, mannered, and strong. You're both gentlemen. You don't have to work at it. You don't put on a show. You're just naturally good guys. I think that's what those two need to see on a regular basis because I'm quite sure what they've experienced is the opposite."

Starlight studied her for a moment then kicked at the grass with the toe of his boot. "She's steel, that's sure," he said. "But she's propped up. I figure if whatever's doin' the proppin' ever goes, she'd wilt right into the ground."

"That's a good analysis, Frank. I think what's propping her up is rage. Winnie too. Except she's a child and she takes on what she feels in her mother. That's why she fights with boys. They represent what's closest to the source of her mother's anger—and her own."

Both men nodded solemnly.

"Shame," Roth said. "Little kid havin' to carry that. Me, I figure any man'd put that in a kid oughta be shot and pissed upon."

"Extreme," Maddie said. "But yes. He would have something to answer for. And I think it's not the result of just one episode. I think Emmy's had a few rotten encounters in her time."

"Half-broke horse," Starlight said.

"Excuse me?" Maddie asked.

He looked at her and there was a welling sorrow in his eyes. "Half-broke. Like when you get a horse through the ground-work then give up halfway through the teachin' him to take weight on him. Always gonna stay half-broke. Half-tamed. Half himself. Half a horse."

"That's a good metaphor for Emmy," Maddy said. "But I was referring to the effect on Winnie."

"So was I," Starlight said.

She looked at him and he stood and stared off across the pasture to the rib of mountain at the end of it.

"Do you think it would help, Frank? What I'm suggesting? Would you do it?"

He put both hands on his hips and craned his neck and arched his back. When he turned he shrugged his shoulders and twisted his torso. He looked at her directly.

"Everything's predictable out there. Natural. Always seemed to me that the best place to learn about trust was out there. You learn to trust it and you learn to trust yourself framed against it. You can move easy out there knowin' your place. Respect comes outta that. So does courage. Humility. Even a rough kinda wisdom. Faith maybe. But I know you come to love it."

Maddie and Roth watched him and waited but he didn't offer anything more.

"You'll do it?" she asked quietly.

"Land wouldn'a taught me nothin' if I don't," he said and then he motioned to Roth and the two men walked away across the yard and began their chore again. Maddie watched them engage in their wordless teamwork and nodded and then rose and made her way to the house to speak with Emmy.

———

She found him splitting wood and throwing it into a flatbed trailer hooked to a tractor. It was warm and he was sweating freely but he looked keenly alive with the work and she stood a moment and watched him. There was purpose to him. It seemed a relentless and mundane task to her but he was centred with it. He was lithe and quick and precise and the trailer was filling quickly. She stepped clearly into view when he bent to retrieve the maul where it lay against a fence post and turned to walk back to the sprawl of rounds waiting to be split. He wiped a forearm across his brow and nodded and walked quickly to the tractor and put his shirt on over the sleeveless single he worked in.

"Emmy," he said and drank from a plastic bottle.

"I remember watching my father when he used to do this work," she said.

"You said he was a farmer."

"Yeah, but he did a lot of other things too. We moved lots. He worked construction, demolition, drove heavy equipment sometimes. But when he fell and cut and bucked for us, he seemed the most peaceful I can recall him being."

"I love it too. Something about taking care of things. The idea of warm, you know?"

"I do. I love a wood fire."

"Eugene is always on me for a furnace. Me? I favour the old-fashioned. House heats up well with the fireplace."

"You related? You and Roth?"

"No. Eugene come on as a hired hand a few years back. Figured it to be seasonal but he stayed through that first winter and when the thaw come it just seemed right that he stay. We seen through a few thaws together now."

"I like him. He's funny."

"He's cut from rough stuff, but he's got a good heart. Tells a good story, works like no one's business. I trust him. He's my friend. Can't see me workin' this place without him now. Fact is, I don't know I'd want to."

She moved closer and stepped over rounds of wood and when she was close to him she righted one and sat on the end of it. Starlight kicked one upright with his boot and sat a yard to her side. They both looked across the pasture. They could see the white shoulders of distant peaks with a deep blue sky standing on them. Cloudless. Calm.

"Why you want to do this, Frank? For Winnie. You don't know us. Seems you done so much already givin' me this work, lettin' us get set up here, get started."

Starlight nodded and looked down at his feet. He made considering his words a physical thing. She watched as he thought, his lips clinched and jaw set firm before he raised his head and scanned the work area and settled his view on the old tractor.

"The man who raised me wasn't my father," he said finally. "My dad was a drunk. He died that way. Never knew my mother. Lost all ties to her when my dad passed. But I never felt no loss in that, never felt deprived, short-changed, cheated. Nothin'. I guess that's on accounta the old man. He brought me up right here on this land. When I was small he started takin' me out there. Horseback. We'd ride and he'd point things out to me and explain 'em as best he could. He taught me how to do things. Set snares, track, fish, hunt, build a lean-to. Boy things. Give me a gun and taught me to use it. He wasn't Indian. But he knew I was and he give me everything he could that was close to that so I'd know something of myself.

"When he got too old and gimped up with arthritis to ride I started goin' out there on my own. Days I'd go. All alone on a horse. Come to love that. Things made sense out there where things in town didn't. Never took to school. Got my education out there. Alone with all of that."

He stood up and walked to the fence. She followed him. He raised an arm and drew her attention along the far flank of ridge and down to where the pasture rubbed up against the foot of it, then across slowly to the barn, the house, and the outbuildings.

"I felt right out there. Free of measuring up, free of what other people thought I might have to be. It was wild but it had order, flow, rhythm. You could learn that if you were out there enough. I was. It hooked me then. It hooks me now. All I ever had of Indian comes from that alone time there. That land and this land is all the ceremony I ever felt a need for. Watchin' the sun come up and set on it become all the prayer I ever felt a need to say. This here is my history. This here is my home. It's alive in me.

"I see you two and I see you lookin' for a place to set your feet down. All fidgety and nervous from the lack of it. Scared, even. I don't know why. It ain't my business to know. But the old man taught me if I can help someone I should. That land give me a place to put my feet down. Figure maybe I can give it to her.

"Thing is, once it fills you, once you come to know it, you never got to feel lonely or lost or sorry no more. You always got a place to carry all that, leave it, let it go. And it comes to fill you again. Me? I figure Winnie could use some emptyin'. You too, if you'll have it."

He turned to look at her. Her eyes were glistening and she turned away from him and raised a cuff to her face and wiped at the corners of them and sniffled. Then she sorted herself. Set her shoulders straight and stood taller and looked up at him. There was a slight quiver to her chin but she was resolute and held his gaze before breaking it off, then walked back to sit on the round again. He followed her. He sat without speaking. She ran her palms along the tops of her thighs and rubbed the small creases of fabric flat. They sat mutely for long minutes.

"There's whole parts of my life I don't remember," she said. "They're gone. Blanked out. I know I never had a home. Not a proper one least ways. Not like you. Never had nowhere to set my feet down. Not as a kid and never as a grown woman. My dad used to touch me. He did that a lot. All kinds of ways. All kinds of ways."

She went quiet. He watched her and to Starlight it seemed as though she got smaller as she sat there on that round of wood. Tinier, helpless, shaky. He felt awkward. He felt too big, too heavy, too rough, too callused. He sat there with his hands folded together and waited her out.

"I had lots of men but Winnie never had a father. Lotsa times they were nice to her to get to me. None of them were ever any good. I got used to that. Kinda thought it was what I was due. That I got dirtied when I was a girl and they could see that. Never had no good guy. I didn't deserve that. I settled for the drunks, the fighters, the lazy, dirty, unpredictable ones. Those I thought I knew because they were most like my dad."

She looked over at him and he could see the struggle it took for her to talk like this. "Bet you're second-guessing choosing to help us out now, ain't ya, Frank?"

"No," he said quietly. "I'm sorry."

"Sorry about what? You ain't done nothin'."

"I'm sorry ya had to go through all that."

She laughed. It was ragged, halfway between a bray and a cackle. "Most of the time I chose it, if ya want to know the truth of it. Chose it because I didn't deserve no better. Once Winnie was born I chose it so she could have a roof and a bed and food. Didn't matter what they did to me then as long as she was gonna be okay. You drink enough you can blank out anything."

"You couldn't though," he said.

"I guess I wasn't as tough as I thought, no."

"Tougher," he said.

"How so?"

"You got her out."

"Did I really? From what Maddie says maybe I can't ever really get her out."

He scratched at the back of his head. "Well, I sorted out a lot of tough stuff on horseback and walkin' on the land. Maybe we start with gettin' her passed fightin' with boys then we can help her get over fightin' with herself."

"And me?"

"You just mount up and see what happens."

"Neither of us ever rode a horse."

"I wasn't talkin' about no horse."

He walked back to retrieve the maul and set a round of wood on the splitting block and swung it in a long arc and struck it cleanly through the wood. She walked back to the house with the dull thunk of the work keeping tempo with her stride.

2

HE TAUGHT THEM HOW TO SIT A HORSE every day after school, walking them along the sides of the stock pen. The girl was excited, happy, and she tried to do what he said. Emmy was grim and determined. She let her head get in the way of the rhythm of the horse. She yawed in the saddle and gripped the pommel to keep herself straight. He needed to know they could sit a horse without difficulty. The girl got there fastest. Emmy fought gamely but her insistence on feeling safe and secure in the saddle kept her back. After a week he believed they were ready for the backcountry trails.

That Friday while they waited for Winnie to return from school he tacked up four horses. Then they loaded gear on a packhorse. It didn't take long. When the girl jumped off the school bus and ran up the lane, they were ready. Once Emmy and Winnie had changed clothes, he tied rain slickers behind their saddles and led them out of the pen onto the hard bake of the pasture.

"Just sit the horse like I showed ya," he told them. "These are good girls you're on. They'll want to go nose to tail behind me, but hold them back some. Don't want them to get too close. Eugene'll bring up the rear with the packhorse. Nice steady line. Have fun. Relax and look around you. We're headed into some mighty pretty country."

They walked acoss the pasture and he dismounted and opened the gate at the edge of a thin trail. When they'd passed through he closed it, remounted his horse, and guided them up the winding path that led up the ridge. He heard Emmy gasp. He glanced back behind him and caught her eye and nodded. She returned it stoicly. The trail had been worn in from years of use and wound between large ponderosa pines and polars. He had to yell over his shoulder for them to watch their legs as the horses edged around the trunks. It took them half an hour to crest the top. He walked his horse close to the edge and dismounted and then helped Emmy and Winnie down.

"You okay? Ya did well there."

"Didn't feel so well," Emmy said. "It took a while to get used to the slope."

"Goin' down's a little trickier but you'll get a feel for it by the time we're back," Starlight said.

"I liked it," Winnie chimed. "My horse just chugged right up that hill."

He smiled at her. "You look like a natural up there."

She smiled back at him and he reached out and rubbed the back of her shoulder. She shied off and he pulled his hand back. Roth caught his eye and squinted. The four of them stepped closer to the edge and looked out across the cuts of scarp and ridge that pushed upward into crest and peaks helmeted with snow. In that hard and fulgent light, the land appeared to divide itself into planes and angles that called attention to its individual parts so that the effect of taking it all in with one sweeping gaze was dazzling. Emmy swooned and Starlight caught her elbow. She righted herself quickly and swiped at the place where he had touched her. Winnie dropped down and sat on a rock and put her chin on her knuckles and stared at the land's array. A breeze wrinkled the silence.

"It's westward here," Starlight said. "I come up to watch sunsets or moonrise sometimes. Makes for a nice walk."

"You walk up that ridge? Thought it took a horse to do it," Emmy said.

"Plumb loco this guy," Roth said. "Some days he'll walk up here and be gone for days with nothing but a knife, a hunk of cord, and a fishing line with a hook. I'd never walk up that thing. Not near crazy enough for that."

"You get used to it," Starlight said.

"I don't see how," Emmy said.

"You might," was all he said.

They all took some water and remounted, and he led them along a twisting path running roughly parallel to the edge of the cliff. The intermittent bursts of view were jaw-dropping. There seemed no separation between land and the oceanic sweep of blue and cloud. The trail dipped, revealing sudden mercury pots of lakes and the sleek turquoise sheen of creeks and rivers rimmed by an undulant carpet of trees. When the trail snaked back closer to the edge of the plummet they were hung suspended over a valley with beaver ponds humped up behind the snarl of trees and rocks and mud that formed their dams. The grass there seemed lush and full and rich. They walked the horses down and when they broke from the trees it was to step out into that long valley. The press of ridge on both sides made them feel coccooned and there was little noise but the whisper of wind through that long, funnelled gap. The air held the fecund tang of bog and sap and gum. He led them along the bottom of the ridge until it broke inward to form a sheltered horseshoe facing outward toward the creek and a beaver pond beyond it. Away to the south and west they could see the regal ermine white of peaks chiselling at a sky so blue it pained the eyes.

"It's like a storybook," Winnie said.

"We're here all weekend," Starlight said.

He flung a leg over the pommel and slid to the ground. Roth took his time and dismounted slowly and carefully. The two of them helped Emmy and Winnie down. While the woman and the girl stood together, transfixed, taking in the spectacle, Roth and Starlight began unpacking the gear from the horse and set to making camp. Roth unfolded canvas and rope while Starlight walked into the trees with a small axe and returned with an armful of stout poles. They sharpened one end of the poles, saving the cuttings and shavings in a pile. Winnie watched them for a moment and then ran off to the edge of the creek, Emmy following her slowly. Starlight and Roth cut strips of bark from the poles and used them to tie pairs of the poles together to form triangles. When they'd chosen the campsite they drove the pointed ends into the soft ground and laid another pole horizontally between the forks at the top ends. Then Roth stood in the middle and held the framework steady while Starlight attached ropes and pulled each tight and staked them into the ground. When they were satisfied that the frame was solid they arranged the canvas over the middle pole and staked out each side to form a tent. They were digging out a fire pit when Emmy and Winnie returned.

"Can we help?" Emmy asked.

"Sure," Starlight said. "Bring some rocks over from the edge of the creek and line this fire pit with them. Nothing too big. Size of bread loaves is good."

They walked off to begin toting rocks while Roth and Starlight set a metal tripod over the pit and placed a wooden box holding pots and utensils and a large iron kettle near the fire. Finally, Starlight and Roth disappeared into the trees with axes and the sounds of chopping and hacking echoed off the walls of the ridge. They emerged with armloads of wood they piled close to the fire. While Roth continued gathering wood, Starlight split the woodpile into burnable chunks. The rest of the camp was set up quickly after that.

"I don't see any food," Emmy said. "What am I supposed to cook?"

"Food all around us," Starlight said.

"Where?"

"Don't mind him," Roth said. "He gets all manly and gruff out here. Wait long enough and he'll show ya what he means."

"Ain't gruff. Out here words don't have the same weight is all."

"Says you," Roth said lightly. "Me, I figger this is where the Injun comes out of ya."

Starlight shook his head. "Maybe so, skinny."

"Skinny?" Roth stood straight and flexed both arms. "You think a body like this happens by accident?"

Winnie and Emmy laughed. Roth winked at them. They laughed louder.

"Well, it just so happens I got me a menu," Starlight said. "Tonight it's trout with mushroom and wild leek salad."

"Where are you gonna get that?" Winnie asked.

"Let's take a walk."

"Out there?" she asked.

"Out there's the best grocery store anywhere. Come see," he said.

He began to walk toward the trees, looping a knife sheath around one thigh. Winnie regarded him with wide eyes and then ran after him.

Emmy and Roth watched them go.

"She'll be okay, right?" Emmy asked.

"I'll tell ya somethin' I know about Frank," Roth said. "If ever there was a man who could keep anybody okay anywhere out on the land, it's him."

Roth set about making a fire while Emmy took the kettle and filled it at the creek and lugged it back. He helped her hang it on the tripod above the flames that were slowly licking at the kindling he'd set in the middle of the pit. He brought a log from the trees and set it on one side of the fire and then returned with another for the opposite side. They sat across from each other and watched as it grew slowly into an orange blaze.

"Frank's a good man," he said. "Best I ever knew an' I known a lot in my time."

Just then Winnie ran out of the bush clutching a bundle to her chest. "Ma, look what we found!" She laid the bundle of greens beside the fire and Emmy inspected them. There were wild leeks and mushrooms and greens she didn't recognize. When Starlight joined them he had a kerchief filled with berries.

"Ta da!" Roth said. "Now for the main course."

The sun was beginning to set. Starlight walked slowly toward the creek. As he got closer he hunkered down and approached it in a slow, stealthy creep. The others watched him and when he waded thigh-deep into the creek they walked toward him slowly, reverently almost, affected by the deep calm that resonated from him. They sat on the rocks beside the stream. He stood bent forward with his hands thrust elbow-deep into the pooling current and waited. When he stood up with a trout in his hands Emmy gasped and Winnie clapped in glee and moved forward on the rocks to get a better look. Starlight tossed the fish onto the bank and turned and repeated the process three more times. Then he waded to the shore with the last fish in his hands, took his knife and gutted them all, before gently releasing the innards into the stream. He clumped an inch of wet clay from the bank around each fish and set them down in the fire.

"Why are you doing that?" Emmy asked.

"Clay bakes," he said. "It's like an oven around the fish. We let the clay cool then crack it open. Best way to cook fish."

"You never heard of a fishing rod or a pan?"

"Heard of them. They're handy enough. More fun this way." He looked at her and offered a small grin. "Old-time skills. They keep you real."

"It's a modern world though."

"Doesn't always have to be."

While the fish baked he gathered thick grass from a boggy patch where a small streamlet trickled off the ridge. He returned to the fire and sat and wove the fronds into a loose mat. Roth had filled a large pot with water and set it to the side of the fire. Starlight placed the mat across the top of the flames and set the greens, mushrooms, and leeks that Roth had cut and sliced onto it. Then he placed the lid over the mat and waited. The sun dropped lower. Shadow began to reclaim the land. Emmy and Winnie sat closer together across from him. They smiled up at

Roth as he placed a wool blanket over them. Starlight stoked the fire and sat back on the log and began to twist a smoke for him and Roth. When he finished, the skinny man sat beside him and they lit their cigarettes with the glowing end of the stick Starlight was using to poke the fire. They smoked silently. Emmy and Winnie hunched forward together, watching the flames.

"It's nice," Emmy said. "Can't recall the last time I had a fire on the land."

"Wait'll you get that grub into ya," Roth said.

"I'm hungry," Winnie said dreamily.

"Soon," Starlight said. "You want to check to see if them fish are done?"

"Can I?" Winnie asked. "But how will I know?"

"Poke 'em with this." Starlight held up his stick. "If the clay is hard they're done. Then you just push them up against the rocks and one of us'll grab 'em out."

"Then what?"

"When they're cool enough to handle we'll split 'em open on the rocks and eat 'em along with them greens that'll be all steamed and ready too by then."

"That's way better than a stove," Winnie said. "More fun."

"Sure is. Eugene and I'll get the plates and stuff."

"Plates?" Emmy asked. "And forks? A little modern, don't you think?"

"Well, a gentleman wouldn't ask a lady to eat with her fingers."

"Or off a rock. You are bringin' me along on this whole gentleman thing, right?" Roth asked.

They got the plates and utensils and then Starlight beckoned Winnie over and handed her the stick. She took it grimly. He walked with her to the fire and when she reached to poke the clay he hooked a finger into the belt loop at the back of her jeans.

"I think they're done," Winnie said.

"Well, haul 'em over to the side."

The girl leaned into the fire again and Starlight maintained his grip on her belt loop. She struggled but got the fish to the rocks.

"Now what?" she asked.

"Now I'm gonna grab my gloves and reach in and haul 'em out."

"Can't I do that?"

"You wanna?"

"Yeah."

"Fire's gonna be hot on your arms. You sure?"

"Yeah."

Roth tossed Starlight a pair of work gloves and he held them open while Winnie slipped her hands in. They were huge and she held them up to her face and giggled. Starlight hooked a finger back through her belt loop and she leaned down and reached for the fish. It was awkward with the huge gloves but she grabbed the first fish with both hands and pulled it free of the fire and dropped it on the grass. She beamed at her mother. When they had all four fish cooling on the grass she ran over and sat beside her mother and stared at the smoking clay.

"Okay," Starlight said. "They should be ready. Come over here with them gloves."

The girl ran over to him.

"Now just lift one of them fish. Grab it around the middle and give it a good crack on a rock. Not too hard though. Just a good sharp whack."

Winnie clenched her teeth and picked up the first fish as he instructed and rapped it on a rock. "It split!" she said.

"Good," Starlight said. "Now do the same thing with the others."

The girl split the clay on all four fish and together she and Starlight peeled them open. As clay fell away there was only steaming flesh. They put each fish on a plate and handed them to Roth, who laid a helping of greens beside the fish. When they had all been served a plate they sat by the fire and ate.

"This is wonderful," Emmy said. "So good."

When they were finished Roth gathered the plates while Starlight gave each of them a handful of berries washed in the stream. They sat silently and ate the berries and stared at the fire and upward at the sky. A wolf howled far off. There was the splash of a fish in the creek. Something small scurried through the brush. The flames licked away at the darkness and in that flush and lambent glow they felt no need of words. The men smoked. The woman and the girl rocked back and forth and the night became a living thing around them. They could hear creatures and night birds and the sudden swoosh and flap of bats hunting insects and when they looked beyond the fire there was the quicksilver seam of the creek radiating moonlight and the shoulders of the trees leaned forward closer toward them. The brawny form of an owl skimmed across at the boundary of the light and the flap of its heavy wings seemed to flay back the skin of the night, and the girl watched it vanish into the sepulchral black and all she could find to say was, "Oh."

Winnie woke in the first faint twitter of morning. The sunlight eked through the skin of the tent and she stood and shivered and climbed into her clothes. They'd slept on a pair of aluminum camp cots. Her mother was gone. The blankets she'd wrapped herself in were in a tumble on the cot and her boots were missing from beside the door. The girl found her own hikers and stepped into them and walked to the door with the laces loose and straggling. She opened the flap and the light and the space hit her hard and she felt vertigo at the huge, open air of it. Her mother sat beside Roth at the fire, looking out intently at the stretch of grass that led to the bush a hundred yards away. She followed her gaze and saw Starlight standing in the open with his head leaned back and his arms held out to his sides, palms up and fingers splayed. He appeared to be sleeping. She eased out of the tent and walked over to her mother and crouched beside the log she sat on.

"What is he doing?" she asked in a whisper.

"Just watch."

He didn't move. He stood there in perfect stillness and the only motion she could see was the slow swell and release of his chest as he breathed. There wasn't a sound except the birds in the trees. Her thighs ached and she slid to her knees. She rested a hand on her mother's arm. The man maintained his posture and the longer she watched the more she became aware of a change in the air, a shift, like a drop in pressure, and she looked beyond him to the trees at the base of the ridge. There was nothing. Then there was a shift there too, a wrinkle, a waver as though the light folded in upon itself. There was a shadow that moved. She saw it in the hard dapple the trees threw around like a slow bleed before form took place and when the deer stepped out fully into the light she caught her breath and squeezed her mother's arm. It was a buck. The rack of him was full and wide and when he lifted his head to sniff at the air the tilt of it was like a basket that caught the light on its tines so that for an instant the morning was impaled there and she had never seen anything so beautiful. The deer eased away from the tree and the man stood in the flat of the field, his hands unmoving in the stillness. The deer stepped silently through the bracken and deadfall and disappeared for a moment in the sweep and range of colour but appeared again, closer, more curious. She began to see the lines of him more clearly, the muscle in sheets and clumps, the roll and angle of shoulder, chest, and haunch, the jut of bone, and she breathed slowly and watched him fill out space. When he got to the line of trees the big buck halted. He stood there and rubbed his horn against a trunk and then eased out into the open. The man did not move. The deer poked his nose upward and sniffed and for a moment she thought he would bolt but he levelled his head and came forward deeper into the indigo flush of morning. He was brown as wet sand. She could see the black of his hoofs in the grass, the nub of nose and lines of it against the flush of white at his chest and in a haired ridge down his spine. The glimmer of wet at his nose and eyes. He moved cautiously through the damp grass and the girl could see his nose working, the ears all pyramidal and taut, moving in soft swivels, and the bunches of muscles in his back legs twitching, ready to bound. But he came forward in an even, measured walk. All the man did was breathe. They were ten feet apart. The deer took to moving forward two steps at a time and halting, waiting, alert. Finally, the buck stepped right to the man and sniffed at the hem of his shirt and along the length of his arm then down his torso before raising his head and looking flush at his face. They stood like that for long moments and the girl held her breath in her throat and when the man raised a hand slowly and put it on the neck of the deer it rushed out of her in a sough and she heard her mother do the same. He held his hand on the deer. The buck stood still, only the flare of his nostrils moving. Then Starlight took his hand away and spread his arms wider and the deer backed up and when he was ten feet away again he turned and walked back majestically into the trees, regal, proud, and disappeared into the shadow.

Starlight turned then and began to walk back to the fire, nodding and keeping his eyes at his feet. He looked up as he neared and there was no surprise or shame to him and Emmy found herself standing as he approached.

"What was that?" she asked.

"Old-time skills," he said.

3

CALGARY ENDED AS IT BEGAN: void of direction, derelict of hope. They worked as itinerant men worked, linking day job after day job, investing more in what night might bring them than the industry of the day, their eyes keen to the quarry. In those nights they toured the dives, booze cans, dance bars, and squalid joints where the amber radiance of liquor allowed the traipse of a fiddle or the rollick of a jukebox to frame them in a degree of light that blinked out quick as consciousness in the twisted tide of beer and rum and whisky. They found like-minded men there. They found women. They entered a community of foundlings, and in the haze of cigarettes and weed and garbled talk, a sort of haven where all beyond the doors was laid aside and forgotten and replaced by a lurching sort of harmony that embraced the candour of desires and yearnings and hungers driven by the very darkness they sought shelter from. In these loose cosmologies they orbited hope together, only to spin off in sad and separate trajectories when the gravity of drink waned and their mass dissolved and the universe became as it was, cold, vacuous, lonely, and forbidding. They drove then. Aimed the truck through ramshackle neighbourhoods where even dogs lay down against the dark and peered at lighted windows in vague trust that she would be illuminated there. She never was.

So Calgary became Edmonton. One lucid morning they accepted two weeks' labour on an oil rig, where they laid the booze aside and worked hard and savagely to earn enough to carry them through a season of searching. There the twelve-hour days and the camaraderie of working men allowed their rage to fester and they emerged hardened by it, embittered, sore, and hungry for release. In the city they found it.

Another room and another fire escape above a scrabbled alley on mornings cold as stone. They were huge and brawny and resonant with a sneering disdain for anything beyond the moment they inhabited. They gathered hard men and loose women around them and for a time it almost seemed enough to stultify the gnawing ache of their scars and the acrid memory of heat and flame and blood boiled into floorboards. But it wasn't. They rose to the flame of vengeance and rancour. They prowled. They sat parked for hours on the strips where pawnshops, pan-handlers, hookers, thieves, and boosters ran. They watched the doors of the welfare offices and hostels and the rooming houses where their cadre of friends advised them the fallen and the broken and the beggared started off or ended up. They found the women's agencies. They trolled schoolyards. Then they looked for men. They searched the Legions where broken, old, and lonesome soldiers went. They found the country bars where the laggard ghost of Hank Williams hunched by a jukebox and scores of sorry stragglers gathered for the twang of heartbreak to assuage their rent and tattered souls. They acquainted themselves with bootleggers and small-bag pushers and anyone with a rough survey of the comings and goings of the street and its people.

"Why we still doing all this, Jeff?" Anderson asked.

"You know how to hunt," Cadotte said.

"Yeah. And that hooks up to this how?"

"You become what you hunt."

Anderson nodded. "But why'nt we just call the cops and report the truck stolen?"

"We don't want no heat around this. Cops get a sniff, suddenly she's picked up then disappears, you know who gets the first eyeball."

"Never thoughta that."

"Become what you hunt. Best way of finding what you're lookin' for."

"What if she changed?"

"Emmy? She ever feel like she could change when you were humpin' her?"

"No. Not likely."

"Follow the game trail then."

So Edmonton became Red Deer and Lethbridge before they began to circle back toward the coast.

4

THE FREEZER ARRIVED FIRST. Roth and Starlight hauled it from town on the flatbed and they installed it at the far end of the mudroom off the porch. They traded a steer for fresh chicken, pork, beef, fish, vegetables, pies, and bread to fill it. The four of them worked together to bag everything properly and for Starlight it was an odd feeling. He'd grown used to taking or buying what he needed when he needed it and the idea of storing and preserving was new and strange. He saw the sense in it. He could determine how it would pay off in leaner times perhaps. But the notion of an appliance was largely lost on him.

So the washer and the dryer they installed in the crawl space beneath the kitchen did little to clear up his discomfit. The new refrigerator and matching stove altered the kitchen he'd grown used to, as did the new countertop, stainless steel sink, and racks of pots and pans Emmy showed them how to hang from the ceiling. The television they set in the living room changed it completely. The woman and the girl and Roth sat around it and became absorbed by the flickering and changing light and the swell and break of sound. He began to store the old man's things in his room and the storage room in the equipment shed.

The new table lamps and chairs replaced the rocker he took to his room and the equipment catalogues and magazines disappeared quickly and there was an order and a sheen to things that baffled him. She asked for money for household things and he gave it to her and watched as the old house transformed around him, the smell of polish and wax and new rugs and drapes and incense gradually pressing back the oil and grease and man smells he'd lived in all his life so that even his sense of smell was disrupted. The changes were abrupt and he struggled to welcome them. But the back porch remained the same and he took his private time there each evening to sit and rock and muse and smoke and watch the land ease out of its daylight boundaries and into the swaddle of night. It was his haven.

Emmy found him there one night soon after the last of the purchases had been installed. "Can I join you?" she asked.

"Yes," he said and indicated the rocking chair beside him. "Nice night."

"Mmm-hmm. I like the quiet. It's never the same twice."

"Not so much quiet since we came."

"Always quiet," he said. "A person's just gotta wanna find it."

"I'm glad I found it. That's kinda what I wanted to talk to you about."

"All right."

"How did you do what you did? Out there. With the deer."

He crushed out his cigarette on the lid of a jam jar and tossed the butt into it before tapping the lid on the rim of the jar and screwing it back on. "I been going to the land alone since I was nine," he said. "I never recollect bein' scared out there or lonely or sorrowful. Instead, I always felt evened out, made right kinda.

You come to know quiet out there. But we know noise moren' quiet after a time an' we figure that's what's normal. It ain't. It's quiet that's normal. Animals get that. They never lost it like us. They move in it. They wear it. It's the normal way of things for them. So after some years I come to understand that if you're lookin' for an animal or you wanna know it, you got to be what you seek."

He leaned his head back in the chair and stared out at the serrated line of ridge and sky. He looked so intensely that she looked too. There was nothing to be seen but sky.

"Quiet, you mean." She said it in a hushed tone.

"Yeah. You gotta learn to wear it. Move in it. Become it. When you learn how to do that you're joined to what creatures know and feel and they ain't scared of you."

"That's when they come to you?"

"Maybe," he said. "If that's your intent. Me? I always just kinda wanna be absorbed into that quiet and pull it into me at the same time. They feel that. That deer was drawn to the quiet. He wasn't drawn to me. I was just a part of it."

"That an Indian thing? A teaching?"

He looked at her calmly. "I don't know about Indian things. I wasn't raised with them. But I come to know the land and how it fills me. I come to know quiet. And I guess, in the end, I come to know something about things like peace and rightness and letting things be."

"I never had much to do with quiet," she said. "My whole life has been about yelling and cussing and hitting and slapping and breaking. Winnie's too."

"I'm sorry about that," he said.

"Can you teach us? How to get to that quiet, I mean. We need that. She needs that. I just don't know how to give it. Or give it so it lasts more'n a few hours anyways."

"It ain't easy," he said.

"We already been schooled in difficult."

He considered her. She held his gaze. They could hear Roth and Winnie laugh at something on the television. He nodded. "Most of it is unlearning what you come to think you need to know. Gotta unlearn what the world calls normal."

"I could do with a heap of unlearning," she said. "And whatever normal is, I don't know that I ever seen it. Ever been it. Neither has Winnie."

"What you can take and what the girl can take is gonna be different."

"I'd be surprised if it wasn't."

"Both of you are gonna feel right uncomfortable."

"I'd be surprised if we weren't."

"Lotta stuff won't make any sense at first."

"I'd be surprised if it did."

"Whattaya want to know right now?"

She looked out across the pasture and let her gaze sweep slowly over the line of ridge. There was the first icy poke of stars in the gathering dark. Cattle kicked the walls of their pens in the barn.

"When do we start?"

5

THE MORNING WAS JUBILANT WITH LIGHT. Emmy rose when she felt him shake her foot and kicked off the blanket and woke the girl, who complained some but rose and followed her sleepy-eyed to the porch, both of them squinting at the hard, brilliant slap of morning. It was chilly and she wanted coffee but he handed them each a cup filled with water and they sat side by side on the edge of the porch and sipped at it, watching him tying moccasins to his feet. They came halfway up his shins. He tucked his pant legs into them then wound a long strand of leather thong around each moccasin and tied them off carefully in a small square knot. They were simple and unadorned. The bottoms were pads of thick felt. He looked up and caught her watching him.

"You make it through today and I'll show you how to make your own. You'll find them better than your city shoes."

He stood and shrugged into a pack and looked down at them. Emmy and the girl finished their water and followed him across the yard, around the back of the barn, and across a pasture to a winding two-track road that led into a small copse of trees. They took it through a clearing and when it ended at a loop he walked them into the depths of the trees. He strode purposefully and they struggled to keep up. He handed them each a banana and muffins she'd baked earlier in the week. The terrain rolled irregularly, broken and chunked by boulders, fallen trees, and thickets of blackberry. He walked them up and down a series of hillocks to a creek that seemed to come out of nowhere. Then he stopped and set down the pack and knelt at the water's edge and cupped a hand and filled it with water and raised it to his mouth and drank. They both mimicked his actions. There were stepping stones in the creek. He walked easily along them and they followed, ungainly and scared. Then he led them back into the wall of trees on the other side. He walked strongly. Winnie alternated between walking and taking little hitch steps and skips to keep up. Their footfalls sounded clangorous, creating small echoes in the trees, and Emmy felt embarrassed. She took to looking at the ground to avoid tripping on rocks and roots and deadfall. They walked a long ways and when he stopped she was sweating and out of breath. Winnie was flushed but appeared game for more. He regarded them calmly. He didn't show the least effect of the walking.

"Any idea where the farm is?" he asked.

"Behind us," Emmy said.

"Everything is behind us. Which direction is it?"

She swept her gaze around and raised a hand and pointed tentatively at an angle behind her. "West?" she asked.

"That's actually north," he said. "We're walking south and the sun is on your left shoulder. That's east. West is easy to find when you know that. Do you know how you got here? Where we are right now?"

"No. I was following you."

"What were you looking at?"

"My feet mostly."

"So what would happen if something happened to me?"

"I'd turn around and walk north with the sun on my right shoulder."

He grinned. "That's good. But if you were looking at your feet you didn't see the land. You don't have any landmarks. Why were you concentrating on your feet?"

"Because I felt like I was thrashing around trying to keep up with you and I didn't want to make noise."

"Did it help?"

"No. The more I concentrated on making less noise, the slower I walked and the harder it was to keep up. And you're right. I didn't see the land."

"Or the deer? The porcupine? The horned owl?"

"Them neither."

"I didn't see them either," Winnie said.

He stepped over to her, knelt, and looked at her and smiled. "Well, the trick is that you have to see to walk. Hold your arms out to your sides with your palms up and one finger raised."

They both did as he asked. "Can you see your fingers?"

"A little," Winnie said.

"Yes," Emmy said.

"That's okay. As long as you can see them. Now, without moving your head or putting your arms down, tell me what you can see from fingertip to fingertip. Both of you." He stepped behind them.

"There's a rock on my far right," Emmy said. "It's got moss on it. There's a tree right behind it and a bunch of grass all bunched up around the trunk. Then there's ferns and small trees about five feet high. Beyond them about twenty feet I guess are more trees. Thicker. Denser. Pines. No, wait. Spruce.

There's a lot of ferns about three feet high everywhere. I see a mountain over the tops of the trees."

"Me too!" Winnie said excitedly. "I can see all that too!"

"How much did you see before?" he asked.

"None of it," Emmy said.

"Even when you looked up how much did you see?"

"Hardly anything."

"No wonder it was hard to walk," he said to Winnie.

"Yeah. I kept thinking I was gonna trip so I looked down most of the time," Winnie said.

"Well, when you practise seein' everything you don't have to look at your feet. All of us learn to walk with narrow vision. But out here you can really learn to see and walk. Now do this."

He pointed to his feet and angled the toes inward. When he stepped forward he barely lifted the foot, merely sliding it over the ground before setting it down in a rolling motion on the outside edge of his foot, from the heel to the toes. He repeated it with the next step and they watched carefully. He motioned them to follow and they both tried to imitate his motions. It was awkward but they crept along that way and Winnie giggled. It felt cartoonish. At any moment Emmy expected him to turn around and point at her following his furtive creep through the bush and erupt in a huge belly laugh at her expense. But he just kept walking. Her muscles began to ache. The unfamiliar plant and roll of her foot asked her to use leg muscles she didn't know she had and she felt the pain most sharply along her shins and under her knees but she kept on with it. Eventually he stopped and turned to face her.

"How did you breathe?" he asked.

"I don't even know that I did."

"You gotta breathe different. Deeper. Longer. It'll calm you, ground you, give you better balance. You're stalking when you do this. I call it my cougar prowl."

"I wanna prowl like a cougar," Winnie said.

"You just did," he said. "A long time ago we had to get food from the land. We were hunters. Stalkers. You gotta get that prowl back. Get back your animal self."

"I got an animal self?" Winnie asked.

"We all do," he said.

"Our inner animal." Emmy almost grinned.

"Yeah. Walkin' right lets you see everything and learn how to move through it without disturbing any of it. Most people walk hard. Out here ya learn to walk soft. Like animals do. Now, what I want you to do is to look out like you done but without raising your arms and fingers."

Emmy raised her head and stared out across the sweep of land.

"See it," he said. "All of it. When you feel like you know what's there, start walking. Keep on walking with your head up, bein' as quiet as possible. Don't worry about speed or pace. Focus on the walkin'. Walk until you can see what's going on out there. Then come back and tell me what that is."

"But what if a bear comes along?"

"If you're walking right you'll see it before you walk into trouble."

"You're sure?"

"I'm not the one who has to be."

She was alone. He had taken Winnie and vanished silently behind her and she could feel their absence. The feeling of the land was like being pinned to it, suspended against it like a found specimen, its space, its place, its function unknown, the panorama jarring in its complexity. She forced herself to breathe and focused on that until she felt her indrawn breaths deepen and lengthen and a sense of calm settle into her belly and the field of her vision became wide and filled with detail. She practised picking out an image from her periphery without turning her head or peering sideways. She did the same with her vision of the ground at her feet and the canopy of the trees above her, with the pocked flank of ridge and scarp and mountain behind them. Her periphery became up, down, left, right, and forward. She'd never seen in this way before. She stood there until she felt certain she had seen the space in its entirety, would recognize this small territory if she saw it again, could paint it perhaps without leaving anything out. Then she began to walk.

Most people walk hard. That's what he'd said. She focused on not disrupting anything. Each plant of her foot was deliberate and she allowed herself to breathe, to relax, to sink into the process of walking and seeing and listening. The view shifted. There were new things at her feet and breaks in the pattern ahead of her and she had to wrestle with the desire to sweep her head around to look at everything. She stopped. She gathered herself. When she calmed she moved forward again and the bush began to open deeper ahead of her and she lowered her stance and crept forward with a stealth that surprised her. Then her foot caught on a root. She rattled small pebbles loose. Branches whispered through the air when she brushed by them and she wanted to curse, to mutter, grouse about her lack of finesse and furtiveness. But she held her silence like a weapon and moved forward. She'd only thought she'd seen what the panorama had presented. Here was a rotted log camouflaged in knee-high grass. There, a rock clumped with moss. An anthill alive with scurry. A raccoon dozing midway up a ponderosa pine. Trees, more than she'd seen initially, lined up one behind the other like troops until she'd moved far enough to see the jigsaw puzzle pattern of their scatter again. Moving forward became a dizzying array of detail in her increased periphery, the vertigo almost overwhelming, and she stopped and sat and breathed and willed herself to calm. When the feeling passed she stood up again and reclaimed the view and began to move. Time ceased its hold. Distance became irrelevant. Speed was an ignored process. She walked. She saw. She recognized. She became a creature again.

It was late afternoon when she stopped. The shadows were long and it made it easy for her to know which way was west so she kept the sun at her left shoulder and moved steadily northward. She passed the place where she began her solo walk and pressed onward. The walking was easier, though her leg muscles complained bitterly. She had to stop less often to reclaim the wider peripheral view. She saw more naturally. When she crested a small hillock of trees and saplings she saw them sitting on a rock, whittling at lengths of saplings. She saw the stripping of bark at the base of the rock they sat on and smiled at her ability to see detail in this new way. It was a few hundred yards to where they sat and she pressed her lips into a grim line and moved intently in the stalk and edged closer. They kept whittling. She crept closer and closer, using trees as a blind and leaning forward from the waist and hunching her shoulders. She could feel the tightness of her breath and fought to relax it at the same time she focused on each placement of the foot and as the distance shrank and Starlight and Winnie remained locked on their knife work she wanted to giggle at her control, agility, and quiet. She felt as though she flowed toward them. She was a dozen feet away when he spoke.

"Wind is at your back. You smell like last night's fire," was all he said and kept whittling.

"Shit," she said. "I thought I did well."

"You did. For a first-timer."

"Anything else I should know?"

"Everything rustles. Out here, where there's nothing to cover sound, you have to choose what you wear."

"But I found you."

"The birds tipped me off first."

"How did they do that?"

"They stopped chirpin'." He stood up and handed her the shaved sapling. It was split at one end into four prongs and the prongs were whittled down to nubby points. "Hard enough to learn to walk proper," he said. "It's lots for one day. But I'll teach you how to fish. We'll finish this when we get to the creek. Did you know that fish choose?"

She twirled the stick in her hands. "Choose what?"

"Where to hang out. There's a lot of water to choose from but they pick what's best and easiest for them. The old man taught me that ninety per cent of the fish live in ten per cent of the water. If you can read water, you'll never go hungry."

Winnie slid off the rock and held up the stick she'd been working on. It looked like his but rougher, less articulated. "Look what I done, Ma."

"That's wonderful," Emmy said. "What else did you do today?"

"We walked. Then we sat in some places. I was real quiet. We got animals to come out so I could see them."

"You did? How did you do that?"

"By bein' quiet. I saw squirrels, some cool birds, a snake, rabbits, and a bobcat."

"You saw a bobcat?"

"Yeah. Frank told me she was out there. He showed me her tracks. Then we did the cougar prowl so we could get close and laid down behind a tree and breathed. That's when she came outta the bush. She stood almost right in front of me!"

"Were you scared?"

"No. Frank said as long as I breathed and stayed quiet she wouldn't be bothered by me. He was right!"

"Did you learn anything else?"

Winnie turned serious. "Yes," she said. "I learned that everything works with rhythm. If I stay quiet, I can feel it. Then, if I can feel it I can start to hear it, and then I can start to see it if I really want to. That's how come the bobcat came."

"Because you wanted to see it?"

"Yeah. But I felt the rhythm first. And Frank said I could learn to smell it too an' even taste it! I wanna be able to do all that. What was that other word again?"

"Sense," he said. "You get so you can sense things."

"Yeah. It means you know without seein'. We're gonna come out lots so I can learn how to sense things."

Emmy looked at Starlight. He met her gaze. She offered a small grin and played with a strand of her hair.

"That's beautiful," she said.

———

When they reached the creek he handed Emmy the knife and directed her to find and cut two twigs half as thick as each of the prongs on the sapling. When she came back with them he showed her how to insert the twigs crosswise so the four prongs were spread apart. Then he took the sapling and thrust it at a stick lying on the ground. When the crosswise sticks snapped the prongs came together and he lifted the captured stick off the ground and held it out to her. "That's a fish," he said.

"Yummy."

He pointed at the creek where it bent before straightening behind the cabin. "You want to look for places where the current slows some but the water isn't too deep. Like coming off that bend there. Can you savvy which side a fish would put up?"

She squinted at the water. "Well, the current would cut the water deeper on the inside of the bend. On the outside it would be calmer and a fish wouldn't have to fight so much to grab any food that was drifting in the current."

He nodded. He took his knife and cut two more twigs off a dead branch of willow by the stream and inserted them between the prongs and motioned for them to follow. He strode around the outside of the bend. There was the humped back of a sand-bar in the middle of the stream and he waded out to it in the knee-high flow and climbed up onto the far end. He pointed to a spot about eight feet beyond it. The water deepened slightly and the current had been split by the sandbar so that it seemed a lazy, translucent green. He stepped into the current slowly and turned to look at them.

"Watch me," he said.

He walked carefully into the slight depth with the stick held above his waist. He turned into the flow with it and switched his grip so that he held the stick at an angle slightly outward from his body. Then he peered into the water and stood stock-still. He barely seemed to breathe. They sat in the sand, watching him. Emmy could feel the breeze in her hair and she practised her peripheral vision so that in his stillness he seemed to anchor the whole sweep of territory and she could almost feel the intensity of his concentration. The swish of the water. Birds. The sun throwing cloud shadow across everything. When it seemed like nothing was ever going to change or move he drove the stick down so fast and sudden it shocked her but left barely a ripple on the surface of the water. When he lifted the stick there was the silver flank of fish gleaming in the sunlight. Winnie laughed and clapped her hands.

He carried the fish to the sandbar and laid it on the ground and cleaned it. Then he carried the offal to the water and laid it gently in the flow and let it go and then looked up at her. "Saavy?" he asked.

"Maybe not the gutting part."

"Your turn then. Both of you."

He handed her twigs to separate the prongs and she took them and waded into the stream with Winnie right beside her. The girl's eyes were ablaze with light. When they reached the spot where he had stood they turned into the current and raised their sticks in the same manner as he had and squinted into the flow and tried to remember to breathe. There was that curious feeling of time losing its value. To Emmy it seemed that she existed only for her breath and the power of her intention. She felt as though she were willing a fish to appear. It didn't. Not for the longest time. She could hear Winnie breathing deeply beside her. They stood there for what seemed like hours. They could hear the water and the sough of the breeze in the trees on the shore, the twitter of birds and the far-off bawl of range cattle. Neither of them broke their concentration. Then, slowly, the fish appeared like lines of shadow, wispy, buoyant, and hung in the current like idle thoughts. They both raised their sticks carefully. She risked a glance at Winnie. The girl had her lips clenched, staring deep into the current. Neither of them moved. They drove the sticks down in the same instant. Emmy could feel hers press against the bottom and when she raised it there was a fish thrashing silver at the end of it. Winnie was laughing out loud. She brandished her stick triumphantly and they ran, stumbling in the current, toward the sandbar. They fell to their knees but kept the fish raised in the prongs. He laughed and they stood and laughed too and clambered out onto the sandbar and held their sticks and the fish out to him. He took his knife out of its sheath with one hand and took the sticks and fish with the other and handed her the knife.

"I can't," she said.

"Part of it," he said. "You become responsible for this life soon's you agree to hunt it."

"But I didn't think I would actually do it."

"You still gotta finish the deal."

"I can't," she said again.

He stared at her with steely, unwavering eyes. "You asked me to teach you this way. Well, this is a part of it. Whether you know it or not you're parta everything. Including that water and this fish. You took it and now you need to honour it. It's going to feed you. You need to clean it. That's the deal."

"Will you show me?"

"Just once." He took the fish in one hand and laid it on the ground. He knelt beside it and eased the tip of the blade at the vee in the gill case. He looked up at her. She nodded. He drew the blade down the length of the belly and the split let the guts ease out and she swallowed hard. He pulled them out with one hand and cut them off the body with the other. He met her gaze. He held them out to her and she reached for them queasily. The slime made her want to retch but she carried them to the water and knelt and laid them carefully in the current like he had and then stood and watched them slip and slide and twist away into the depths. She rinsed her hands in the stream and walked back to him, wiping them on her jeans.

"That was good," he said.

"Yeah," she said with an exhale. "I get it now."

"Okay," he said. "Your turn, Winnie."

The girl took the knife and brandished it clumsily but he guided her hands and she pressed on with clenched lips. When she reached in and yanked out the innards she was grave and he admired her intensity. She carried the offal to the shore and laid them in the water. She knelt there and watched them spin lazily in the current and drift away.

"Thank you," she said quietly.

Roth had set out on horseback with the packhorse that morning to organize the camp. As the afternoon had lengthened he lit the fire, and after they reached the camp they ate the fish with rice Starlight wrapped in broad leaves and steamed along with mushrooms over the fire. It was simple, plain, bland, but tasted like an ornate feast to her and when she washed it down with water she was amazed at the degree of her fullness, her contentment. She sighed. She scrabbled down and lay with her back against a rock and looked up at the purple-swaddled world. Roth added wood to the fire and they felt the darkness ease down around them and in that quality of silence she could hear the land and it was the only language she needed then. Winnie lay down at her side with a blanket and she wrapped an arm around her and together they took in the parabola of stars. It was deep night when Starlight rose and strode into the bush.

"Where's he going?" she asked.

"You ever get to figure that out you tell me," Roth said. "He finds himself out there."

"More'n on the farm?"

"Farm's where he lives. This is home."

"I don't know how he can just get up and walk out there. Without a gun, I mean."

"Sometimes I sat here days before he come back. Couple times I just packed it all up an' headed in alone. He come out after a few more days. Walked out. Right to the farm."

"He ever say what he does all alone all that time?"

"No. But I heard a word when I was growin' up an' they forced us to go to church. Communion, it was. Never found a place for that word to sit rightly in my head. Not 'til I met Frank least ways. It seems to me that communion means gettin' right with somethin', gettin' close to it. Feelin' like every part of ya fits with it all. That's what he does out there. Communion."

She stared at him across the fire. Winnie slept with her forehead against her ribs. She breathed lightly to not disturb her. "I never felt right with nothin' all my days," Emmy said.

Roth nodded and poked at the fire. "Might be that's how come you're here."

"You think?"

"Hell, I don't know. Frank's the one who can figure things. Deeper things. But me, I guess that there's a mystery to things, to life, and sometimes it just takes charge, ya know? Sometimes it brings the right people to the same place at the same time. Brung me to Frank. Life ain't been the same since that day."

"You think it's God?"

"Can't say. Me an' the notion of God parted company some time back. But somethin's goin' on and that big jasper strollin' around out there in the dark? I kinda often feel he's the one meant to lead me to some notion I can live with."

"I never known no man like him," she said.

"You'n me both," Roth said.

6

THE ENSUING DAYS BECAME JOURNEYS of enrichment and Emmy felt the first bloom of love in her like the first tendrils of spring in the air. She learned to walk into the land fully open and it entered her and she felt tearful and joyous at the thrum and current of it coursing through her being. For days they simply walked. Every step they took in that great wide open was another entry they made together, another passage she made to that odd sense of fullness and emptiness that occupied her belly at the same time. The land. It welcomed her, filled her, and she felt lonely for it when they returned to the farm.

Winnie blossomed before her eyes.

She marvelled at Starlight's patience with the girl as much as she shook her head in wonder at Winnie's capacity to trust him so easily. She wanted to weep at that. Men had never treated Winnie as a little girl. They'd treated her as an inconvenience, something to be endured in their pursuit of her mother, something to be suffered through in exchange for what Emmy could give them as a woman. Winnie had never known a man who asked her questions and then listened to her answers. She'd never been shown things in a way that she could understand. All she'd known was aloof, cold, and distant men who shunted her aside, discounted her, ignored her, and treated her mother as a body, a possession, a commodity right in front of her. She'd seen things that no little girl should ever have to see and it was from a deep well of shame that Emmy watched Starlight move Winnie gently toward a sense of herself framed against the context of the land.

"Did you know that we're movin' even when we're sitting down?" she asked one evening.

"I'm pretty sure I didn't know that," Emmy said.

"Frank told me. He said if I look up at the stars long enough I can see 'em move. It's because the earth is spinning they seem to move. But really it's us."

"That's interesting."

"Yeah but what's real interesting is that we're spinning way fast an' we don't even feel it."

"I don't feel like I'm spinning over here."

"That's cuz we don't think about it. It just happens. Frank said it's the same as when we're on the land an' we stop and sit an' breathe. We're movin' then too but we don't know it."

"How are we moving then?"

"'Cause everything else is."

"I don't get it."

Winnie giggled. "Me neither at first but Frank's real good at tellin' things. He said everything is alive. So everything is movin'. We just think things are still. But if we learn to sit with things we can get so we can feel them movin' even if it's just in a small way at first. If we learn to be real still an' quiet we can feel like we're parta all that movin' and it's a part of us."

"Do you feel that?"

She shrugged. "Only a little. But I'm gonna sit on the land or walk it like Frank does so I can feel it more. You know why?"

"No," Emmy said. "Why?"

Winnie looked at her and her eyes were so clear and brilliant they were like the sky and she felt as though she could fall into them and keep right on falling endlessly.

"'Cause when I get so I can feel it all the time, I'm gonna feel like I'm a part of everything and everything is a part of me—and I won't ever feel lonesome no more."

Within a week Emmy could walk more quickly. Soundlessly. She could close her eyes and feel the faintest breeze on her skin and move into it. While Winnie was at school, Starlight taught Emmy to crouch deeper and still make good forward progress. The muscles at her thighs and knees and lower back complained but she crept for hours that way. He taught her to waddle. The back of her heels were right at her butt and she duck-walked through bush and grass and dry rock and tinder until she could do that soundlessly as well. Then he taught her to crawl. She learned to use her elbows and knees for purchase. She learned to use the tips of her toes, her forearms, the insides of her knees, and the bottom edges of her fists to clamber forward. She learned to do it backwards and forwards without disturbing the ground, without leaving sign of her movement. He taught her how to move through all of these positions and movements and still retain a rhythm, a tempo, and through all of it to maintain an acute awareness of everything around her.

When they were out on the land her days began and ended in silence. They seldom spoke. Instead, she learned to direct her attention to his hand signals, his eyes, his posture, so that cooking and chores and normal acts of living could be dispensed with and shared wordlessly. It amazed her how little she required talk and language. Her words sat in her like stones. When she used them at all she recognized their heft, their significance, their import, and she felt a deepening judiciousness in her choice of them. She came to prefer non-verbal interaction. She came to recognize that every word had a silence between it and the next one and that it was within those minute silences that the real communication happened. She felt like an articulate, sentient creature carrying the language of the wind.

One day they lay in a frail drizzling mist watching eight deer grazing in a meadow. He reached into the pack beside him and removed the camera and a long lens. She touched his elbow and motioned for the unit. He looked at her questioningly and then handed it to her. She made the sign for sneaking on an angle into the wind and around the deer to the far edge of the meadow and he nodded. When he moved to join her she held up a palm and gave him a stern face. He studied her briefly, then blinked. She wriggled backwards, then eased up to a deep crouch and scuttled deeper into the trees and began to crouch-walk around the edge of the meadow. The deer were oblivious. She rose and walked into the wind until she could smell the deer and then dropped back into the crouch to creep closer and finally slunk down on her belly and moved furtively forward to a point where she could see them clearly. She wasn't aware of breathing. She raised the camera to her face and peered through the viewfinder and pulled the deer into focus. A doe and fawn raised their heads to peer off sideways at a sound in the trees and she pulled the focus tight and caught them in profile. She watched them for a while longer then made her way back to where he waited and they rose and walked silently away from the meadow. That night he gave her hide and taught her to cut thong. Then he gave her a thick swatch of felt and showed her how to make her own moccasins.

"You earned these," was all he said.

She sewed through the night. With each stitch she envisioned herself walking. She saw herself at the moist edges of marshes and amid the loose, dry scuttle of pine forest. She felt the breeze on her skin and the fluttery feel of light rain. She imagined easing through the darkness, through depths of shadow so utter they felt like holes disappearing into the earth, and then regal steps into the jubilant spill of morning, sunrise sudden against everything like a tempera wash, the jewelled look of things dazzling to her. When she finally held the finished moccasins in her hands, the idea of walking had become, in their creation, like stepping into a foreign country, the only maps necessary the soles of her feet. She fell asleep with them crushed to her chest.

Then he taught her to run. They were walking along the edge of a bog lined with scrub pines and pokes of spruce. He raised one hand and stopped. She was behind him. He dropped lower with his weight in his thighs and began to jog with his arms swinging lightly, parallel to the line of his thighs. She mimicked him. She could see how the motion helped him maintain a silent gait and she worked at not breaking it with her clumsy first effort. They carried on that way around the bog and she could feel the sear of effort in her legs but willed herself to keep moving in the dog-like trot. When he turned suddenly and veered into the trees she almost collapsed but righted herself and hurried after him, watching the way he planted his feet and copying the roll of them in the crackle of gravel, rock, and grit. He ran that way for a half-hour. When he stopped she leaned against a tree and hauled breath deep into her. He hardly seemed affected by the effort. When she'd recovered he motioned for them to continue and led them deeper into the bush. The running was harder now. There were tall ferns and downed trees and bramble and sudden fissures in the rock she fought to leap over and still he kept up the relentless pace. The moccasins felt loose on her feet but they did nothing to combat the ache and cramp she began to feel in her legs. But she kept on. He ran them up a long curl that topped a ridge then slowed and rose to his full height and walked to a stone at the edge of the ridge and sat looking out over the vista. She plopped down beside him with heaving lungs and a faintness in her head. It took her long minutes to calm.

"We run like hunters, prowlers, searchers," he said. "The purpose of running is to run."

"Isn't that obvious?"

"Not so much. I talked to an old guy one time outside the feed store in town. He was one of the first Indians I ever talked to. We were watchin' some young kids runnin' around the schoolyard. He said that for his people, runnin' was breathin' in the breath of all things. Running was addin' our breath to things. To everything. Some of their runners would run for days."

"What now?"

"Now you learn to run like a creature."

"How do I do that?"

"By not running."

"Jesus."

He laughed. "I hear you," he said. "But if you watch creatures, especially the hunters, they spend most of their time trottin' or lopin' along. They move in starts and stops. They hardly ever run at full speed. Even horses. You can't gallop a horse for hours. Most of the time you're walking or going at a light trot. Dogs too. For them and for wolves, top speed's gotta have a reason. You gotta be able to run like a wolf. Prowlin'. Easy."

"That's how you get close to them, isn't it? Running like that. Like a creature."

"That's part of it."

"What's the other part?"

"Lovin' the feel of the running."

Then he stood up and ran. She followed him. She dropped lower and loped in the low, almost casual way he did and held the pace and began to use her eyes and ears and nose so that after a time she wasn't aware of moving farther as she was aware of moving deeper into the territory she moved through. She saw it. She heard it. She smelled it. She sensed it. And after numerous miles when he stood upright and ran faster through a small ocean of meadow she broke too and they ran full tilt together across that sunlit expanse and into the trees on the opposite side. Laughing.

They ran for weeks. He'd lead her uphill or through long undulating courses along the banks of rivers and streams. They ran plateaus and meadows. They ran from the barn across the pasture and up the curling trail of the ridge. They ran in the evening and they ran in the morning, and she learned to love the feeling of her body in motion. It awakened her to herself. It made her feel keenly alive and so it became like a drug she needed every day and she took to long loping rambles on her own along the concession line that led to town, turning at the Welcome sign to run back. She ran the trails he led her to. Alone. There was no fear in that. Instead, she approached the running the same way she approached the walking and let herself slip into the mystical dream of it, each footfall, each step, each stride a moving deeper into the land and into the country of her own being. She had nights of deep, unmoving, dreamless sleep. She always awoke replenished. Her muscles grew taut and strong and resilient. He showed her how to jump and leap and not break pace, and she began to trust her balance and her lithe strength so that the running became less arduous and more natural, freer, and expansive to her spirit.

"I know why wolves howl," she said one night while they sat on the porch.

"Why's that?" he asked.

"Because it's the only way they can say how it feels."

"Bein' a wolf, you mean."

"Well, yeah. I guess. But when I'm running I feel the world movin' through me more'n I feel me movin' through the world. There's no words for that. There just isn't. In those moments, the only thing I want to do is howl."

7

THERE AROSE IN CADOTTE THE NEED for solitary prowling. He would sit at the edge of his bed and lace up his boots while Anderson watched and then stand and shrug into his jacket and walk silently out of the room and down the stairs of whichever rickety hovel they sheltered in. There were no words for either of them then. Each understood the smoulder of a seep and bleed beyond words, how it roiled the gut and gripped at the temples as relentless as an encroaching madness. The fire had laid embers in each of them. In Cadotte they flickered harder, brighter, drove him with a banked heat that not even Anderson wanted close to when it rose unaided by booze or talk. So he let him walk. Where he went and what he did was no account to Anderson. There were stories even brutal men had no need to hear.

The truck was no use to him. He wanted the feel of prowling. He wanted the firm set of his feet on concrete and the unfailing push of his energy toward whatever doorway his feral instincts took him. He wanted the sense of motion. He wanted the rise of his hackles in the hunt. The hunch of his shoulders. The bristle of energy in him that brought him eventually to a stillness foreign to those who saw him. His bulk was dwarfed by the implied threat, the primal lurk of him sitting, watching, waiting, silent, set down like a malevolent boulder scarred by unknown impacts. Men let him be. Women, certain women, were drawn to him and it was these he stalked, these he allowed beyond the gaping maw of his hate and downward into his darkness.

When he found them he commanded them just as he had controlled her when they met the first time. Baleful. Terse. Urgent. A geyser shaking earth with its mounting pressure. He revelled mutely in their fear and quaking hold on security, their notions of safety and the inexorable slide into the vortex of his unyielding bitterness and contempt. He took them. He demeaned them. He let them feel his power, his control, his dominance. There was no emotion, only a primitive grunting and finish. There was no elegance. He took them in alleyways, the back seats of their cars, riverbanks, parks, deserted areas slung with rusting hulks of appliances and cars. All that mattered to him was the final act of ruthless disregard: the tossing away, the sneering indifference he threw over them in their slumped and shamed departures. He owned them then. He revelled in that. Then rising to his full height he would shrug back into himself and walk through the detritus of a sleeping city, rich in the fumes of its decay, redolent with the after-taste of abandonment, neglect, and ruinations real and imagined and feared. He existed for those nights of triumph. Striding through the dank shadows, it was her face that drove him. The memory of her body, her touch, the languid feel of her half-drunken sprawl across his skin, and the flat, broad thrum of his palm burning with the hate of it and the searing flush of flame and heat and scorch that drove him onward, deeper into the night.

8

"THIS PLACE SEEMS TO HAVE QUIETED down a lot," Roth said.

They were oiling and lubricating the tractor, baler, and wagon in preparation for harvesting the first crop of hay. It was warm and they drank frequently from a large jug of water and the feel of the work lulled them like it always did, that curious sensation of industry, the care and attention to detail, of looking after machines, allowing them to drop lower into a calm, assured set of movements like poetry. They hadn't spoken for some time.

"Hopin' Maddie's seein' change at school in the girl," Starlight said.

"Seen her at the post office day or so ago. She seemed good and pleased enough."

"That's good. I wonder sometimes."

"'Bout what?"

"Whether all we're doin' is enough."

"All you're doin'. Me, I'm along for the ride."

"Couldn't do none of it without you, Eugene."

"Yeah, well, that's big of you to notice that. Ain't like me to bark my own praises. Shy, retirin' sort that I am."

Starlight chuckled. He laid the lubricating gun down at his side and turned his head and looked over at Roth under the wagon. They were both content to lay there without moving.

"I'm gonna need ya to be around us lots when we go out again on the weekend."

"You know I'm all in on that."

"I know. I'm just sayin'."

"I figured you was movin' toward some degree of import."

"How's that?"

"Well, ya get kinda high-strung when there's weighty matters comin'."

"High-strung? I don't know as I ever felt wired up, ever."

"Ya get that way. Ya do. I known ya three years, Frank. We share the same roof, sit by the same fire. I'm savvy enough after all that time to know the signs."

"Oh, so there's signs now, is there? I'd be pleased to know what they might be."

"My pleasure. Good for you to know that there's someone eyeballin' yer behaviour now and then. And me I got a shrewd, calculatin' eye, myself."

"And this shrewd eyeball tells you what?"

Roth turned his head and gazed directly at him. He rubbed at the nub of his chin and smeared a run of grease across it. "See, the thing is, ya gotta learn to read a man like ya would a woman. Now, yer normal women got a run of pure inconsistencies to 'em. Like the bush ya haul me out into all the time. I'll give ya credit that you got a way with the land that's right uncommon and that's good, but ya ain't got such a good eye toward how ya walk about it. Same thing as a woman. Savvy?"

Starlight smiled despite himself. "I'm not real sure I do, no."

"Well, try'n follow along best ya can," Roth said and winked. He rolled over on his side and tucked an arm under the side of his head and stared at Starlight earnestly. "I know it might be hard for you given the startlin' depth of pure thought I lean toward every now and again. But here's the thing. Ya watch a woman. Now she's all concerned about how yer watchin'. It's how come they attach so much to lookin' pretty. On accounta she know's yer eye's on her. That keepin' tuned to you and keepin' tuned to herself leads her to make all kinds of moves that tell you who she really is. Same as you."

"Same as me how?" Starlight asked.

"Well, fortunately for you you ain't pretty, so you never had to pay no particular attention to that part of this equation."

"Yeah. I feel real good about that."

Roth nodded. "But what ya do is wonder if the moves ya make are the right ones. Makes ya all grave and serious. Ya lose that sparklin' youthful glow ya normally carry. Like when yer tryin' to suss where to drop your night line fer fish. A devil-may-care guy like me who just knows he's pretty wouldn't get all scrunched about the eyeballs like you do about it. I just throw a worm on the hook and toss it on out there. But you got to determine what to do. And that's when yer easy to read."

"Scrunched about the eyeballs?" Starlight smirked.

"Yeah, yeah. That's one of yer tells, yeah."

"I'm glad to know ya can know me so good."

"Told ya. Shrewd and calculatin'. And it leads me to knowing here that whatever it is you're thinkin' is best is generally gonna be the best. So stop worryin' it sore."

"I haven't told ya what I'm gonna do."

"Ain't no need, pal. You got you one pure outta this world knowin' about the goin's on of the real world. That world out there, I mean. Beyond them hills. I figure you just stick with what works an' you ain't ever gonna be off the mark."

"Stick with the one what brung ya?" Starlight asked with a grin.

"Now, see," Roth said and pointed a finger at him animatedly. "That there is pure genius. Yer ability to hear wise words when they're spoken around ya."

Starlight shook his head and turned to the work again.

They prepared to ride off in the dying heat of late afternoon. The sun was sweeping downward into a deeper yellow and the horses were excited and Emmy could feel the energy of them as she stood by the fence and watched him pack the second mare. They weren't taking much. He'd told her they were heading out to wilder country and the seeming lack of necessities worried her. She found herself staring outward at the thick mat of forest that covered the ridges and the shoulders of the peaks and wondered what it would feel like to step completely out of the world, to feel the scarp of mountain shut you off from everything you recognized and the quiet of things seeping into you like a draught in an empty room. It scared her some but she shook it off. When he walked the horses over she stepped up on the rail and mounted the mare and sat calmly waiting on him to help the girl up. When they were both settled Starlight and Roth made final preparations and closed the door on the barn and walked over to their mounts and stepped up on the stirrup and swung their legs over in tandem and sat blinking in the slanted beam of the sun. They nudged the horses forward together and walked through the gate and out onto the small green plain of the pasture. Roth leaned down to close the gate to the pen and looked at her and arched an eyebrow and nudged his gelding forward. Her mare tucked in behind and they walked out across the field. Winnie rode behind her and Starlight brought up the rear. There was no wind. The hard bake of the pasture pulled beads of sweat from her and she wiped her forearm across her brow and settled deeper into the languid walk of the horse. Ahead of them the trees sat resolute and the shadows were deep and thick as smudge marks. The motion of the horse lulled her and she sat relaxed and slouching and turned back to look at Starlight, who measured her from toe to chin and nodded and gave her a small grin. He chucked to the gelding and pulled up beside Roth and the walk quickened. When they reached the trailhead they trotted along the curving slant and she felt the land become wild around her.

They climbed around the ridge and then down the other side and into the steep vee of a gully that ran whitish blue with a small stream. All she could hear was the rush of water. The horses picked their way along and the boulders that were strewn along the shore were large and rounded by the force of the current from spring melts. The farther they followed the stream the more she came to hear the silence beyond the rush of water. She looked up and the tree tops cut the sky into a serrated edge. The spruce and fir grew thicker and the talus boulders gave way to smaller, variegated stones and pebbles and gravel. The bed of the stream dipped into an abrupt angle and she had to lean back on the horse to hold her seat. It was a long traverse. Eventually the trail levelled out and they snaked downward and out into a broad valley that was surrounded on all sides by mountains, and the stream bellied out wide and smooth and languid, then pooled and became dotted with beaver lodges and spotted with juts of alder and birch and willow, and she thought she had never seen anything so beautiful.

The sun was a slip of itself against the western cut of mountain. There was a golden light to everything that eased downward to orange and crimson and a hint of the profound purple to come. Starlight walked the horses deeper into the valley and stopped them at the head of a wide pool. She could see fish finning in the shallows. There was the ghost of an old fire ring and he dismounted and walked to it and kicked at the grass that poked up around it. She slid off the back of the mare and stood there looking at everything. While she and Winnie walked to the edge of the stream Roth and Starlight tied the horses to a clump of willows and hefted the stones out of the fire ring and reassembled them atop the twitches of grass. When she looked at him he hooked a thumb toward the trees and they followed him, stepping over logs and rocks and clumps of bushes thick with berries and flowers. He carried a small hatchet and a knife, and they walked to a copse of saplings that he chopped down. When they had an armful they walked back.

He directed them wordlessly. He showed her and Winnie how to strip the bark in long thin strips and then how to use the strips as rope. They pitched the frames of lean-tos and then pulled swatches of fern and cut branches from spruce and willow and laid them across to form the roof.

"We sleep under these?" she asked.

He nodded and they walked off to gather firewood. He led them out to the bush and showed them what to gather and they returned to the camp with armfuls of twigs and bracken. He showed them how to press it all into an oblong like a hornet's nest and set them down in the middle of the fire ring. When he helped Winnie put a match to hers it flared and she laughed when the flames caught. He showed her how to add bigger pieces of wood to it and the fire crackled to life and they stood around it, all orange and wavering in the dying light. He used an alder sapling to make a spear and got them four fish for supper. She cleaned them and flayed them out on forked sticks to cook while Roth and Winnie gathered herbs for a salad.

They ate in silence. The night descended around them. Emmy built the fire back up as he directed and they leaned on logs while he whittled at a piece of dried wood.

"I've been on campouts before," Emmy said. "But I never knew how much you could do with so little."

"The old man used to say the land'll always teach ya what you need to know," Starlight said.

"Do you miss him?"

Starlight studied her a moment then laid his knife and whittling stick at his feet and leaned forward and gazed into the fire. "I don't know as I do. We come out here so much together the things I know and love about it are all connected with him. I can't feel the wind on my face without thinkin' he's touchin' me. Can't hear a moose bawling across a distance without thinkin' he's speaking to me outta that. Them kinda things. I kinda figure he's a part of all that. So I come out here and I get comforted."

"Sounds like you loved him a lot."

"Like I said, he was my father even if he wasn't my real one."

"Why you call him the old man then?" Emmy asked.

"I guess I don't figure *father* to be something you cram into one box that'll hold the word for ya. I figure it comes to mean different things to different people. Me? It means he was my best friend. Always."

"Because he gave you the land?"

Starlight raised his head. She met his gaze.

"Yes," he said softly. "Starts with that, yeah."

"I never met my daddy," Winnie said suddenly. "Or my grampa."

They all turned to face her. She sat beside her mother, leaning forward toward the fire with her forearms on her thighs.

"I think they'da thunk ya were a pretty special kid," Roth said.

"I don't wonder what they looked like," Winnie said. "But I like to wonder how they sounded when they talked. Like how they'd sound talkin' to me around this fire."

"Likely sounded all worldly an' wise like me," Roth said.

Winnie laughed and turned to look at him. "You're funny," she said. "I think they would have sounded like you."

Roth scratched at his ear. "Hard burden to bear. Rumbly, manly voice like mine."

She laughed again. "See?" she said and looked up at Emmy.

"I do see," Emmy said. "I think it's okay for you to choose how you would want them to sound."

"Like Frank then. And Eugene."

"Do you miss 'em?" Starlight asked.

It was her turn to regard him. "No," she said.

He studied her. "Okay," he said.

"I feel the wind on my face, it's just the wind," she said, and Starlight nodded.

———

He taught them to listen. They walked out in silence, leaving the horses behind at the camp. They walked across the valley and up into the heart of the backcountry, and she could feel the nature of things begin to reshape, rearrange, and reorder themselves so that by the time he stopped the land had become a pelagic roll of greens and greys, browns, purples, black, and undulant earthen shades she found no name for in her head. Everything was the same in all directions. Yet everything was different everywhere she looked. She felt lost in its immensity, shrunken, diminished, pitiable almost and she found she could barely breathe. He led them halfway up a slope that looked out over the territory they'd just walked through. She could see the glint of the stream wending its way toward their camp, a shim of tinsel beyond the thick clasp of trees. He sat and the three of them eased down beside him.

"You paid attention coming through?" he asked.

"Yes," Emmy said.

"So you know what's out there."

"Some. There's more I likely missed."

He nodded. "You can't see everythin'. Every sense we got is limited somehow. It's only when we use 'em together that we come to recognize things. Can you see right across the valley?"

"I can."

He looked at Roth and Winnie and they nodded.

"Good. Take a good hard, deep look. Take your time. Sweep your gaze across it. Try'n know it with your eyes. When you feel like you have the whole thing recognized, close your eyes. Breathe. Long an' deep an' slow. Imagine there's a point of light between your eyebrows. Focus on that. Push your attention toward it. When you feel like you're there, in that space, start listenin' to the sounds around you. Don't force it. Stay in that small space and just listen."

The three of them closed their eyes.

"When you figure you can hear everything around you push your hearing outward. Try'n listen farther out."

Emmy closed her eyes. She felt him move into a more comfortable position beside her and she did the same. She heard him breathing, long, slow draughts, and she copied his rhythm. It took some effort but she found the small space on her forehead he'd described. She willed her concentration to that spot. She breathed deeper. Then she began to listen.

She heard the breeze rustle the leaves of the aspens and poplars. She heard it nudge its way through the grass and ferns. She felt herself pushing harder through that spot on her forehead and she heard bees and the tiny claws of chipmunks on bark and a stone loosened by the passing of some other larger creature roll briskly downhill and stop abruptly against another. The knock of it audible as a finger snap in an empty room. She heard birds hopping from branch to branch. She heard all of that. Then she willed her hearing outward beyond the downed log twenty feet in front of her. Then forward, deeper into the trees. There were even more sounds and she nudged him with her elbow.

"Okay," she said.

"How did it feel?"

"It felt like the inside of my head got bigger."

"It did. It got bigger because you let yourself hear deeper. We think we hear what's going on around us but we're only hearing a little of it. When you push out your listenin' you start to really hear things."

"What's the difference?"

"You don't have to do nothin' to listen. Sounds gets to us any-how. You can listen to someone while you're doing dishes, say. Or you can listen to the radio while you're doin' a chore. But when you push your listenin' out, you can hear everything. I kinda figure it's on accounta ya open yerself up to it all."

"What happens then?"

He smiled. "You get connected to what you hear. You become a part of it. It becomes a part of you."

"Is that why you say you're never lonesome out here?"

"Ya can't be when yer a parta somethin'."

"We get to be a part of all this?" Winnie asked.

"When ya really learn to listen. When you can push your listenin' out and really hear where ya are, yeah," Starlight said.

"Then let's push out some more."

They all closed their eyes. Emmy breathed. She found her calmness. She focused on that tiny point of light and pushed her hearing out through it. She pushed it beyond the downed log and through the trees. She heard animal movement, bird-song, the creak of trees, the gleeful babble of water from a spring coursing over rocks and the sibilant whisper of the breeze over everything. She pushed her hearing out over the tops of the trees and over the wide expanse of the valley. She breathed deeper and slower. Her focus on that point on her forehead grew stronger and in her mind's eye she saw the expanse of land she'd looked across. She heard it. From the low bawl of a moose to the grunt of a bear busy clawing at a rotted log to the piercing call of a red-tailed hawk circling far away and downward where the wind claimed its susurrant channel through the deep cut of the valley. She heard all of that. Then lower sounds like running water, a creature digging in sand

and gravel, and the distant drone of an airplane to the south and west of them. The more she let herself become open to sound the clearer her vision of the valley became. In its wholeness it was immense. She could feel it fill her and she pushed harder, willing herself to hear even more of it. Her breathing deepened and lengthened and she fell into a calm place where nothing existed but the kinetic life of that valley in her ears and chest, and she spread her arms wide as though to embrace it and there was the blue of the sky in her and the poke and jut of tree and rock and the checkerboard play of light and shadow everywhere at once, and she could only sigh and the only word she found was "Yes."

Listening drew her to the land alone. She took to leaving a small rucksack that carried cord, matches, a blanket, a plastic bag of tinder, a jar of water, and a ration of seeds and nuts close to the fire. Sometimes, when Winnie was at school, Emmy would loop a knife through her belt and gather the pack and walk away. He never said a word to her. Using the skills he'd taught her she would just walk. She would stop now and then and listen. She practised sending her hearing out until she could do it automatically and hear the things going on around her. It began to take her less time to find that calm centre. Soon it became a matter of closing her eyes and sinking into it. Then it became a chosen act of awareness and she could send it out with her eyes wide open and hear the land fully. She heard bears and walked around them. She heard rabbits and foxes and small game. She heard the tentative caution of deer rustling branches in their furtive passing. In those moments she felt keenly alive and the land seemed to sing to her. Each movement and motion she discerned was like a separate note in a grand composition and all she wanted was to feel swept up in its grandeur. She'd never known this symphony existed before and she drank it in like an elixir. Coupled with its visions and smells, the land was intoxicating in its richness, and she could spend long hours alone with it before returning to the farm and sitting wordlessly on the porch while Roth and Winnie watched television and Starlight sat with her in a stillness that allowed the lowing of cattle, the call of night birds, and the slip of the wind along the eaves to pass through them.

"This is what it's about, isn't it?" she asked one night. "This feeling. This sense of being connected to all of it?"

"Yes," he said quietly.

"But it wasn't about the land, was it? You were teaching me to listen to myself."

"I was."

He seemed to move in his stillness. There was a shimmer to him. She let her gaze drift upward and in the cast of stars against the deep push of space she saw the same otherworldly coruscation, a glimmer beyond all light. He was facing her when she looked back at him. There was a hard obsidian glint to his eyes and the fading purple light threw shadows on his face so that his whole countenance seemed like the face of an old shaman, and she caught her breath.

"I never listened to myself before," she said.

"I know. Few do."

"That's the real wilderness then, isn't it?"

"I reckon it is."

"Can you find your way through that?"

"Me? I guess."

"And me?"

He kept his gaze on the stars. "I don't know. I got no head for how women are."

"Because you never knew your mother?"

"Yeah, that's a big part, yeah. Grandmother neither. Girlfriends too."

"You never had a girlfriend?"

"Never seemed right for me. I was always busy. I never learned to talk to girls. Grew up in a male way mostly."

"So you never . . ."

He looked at her and she could see the discomfort slide over him. Then he shrugged and stood and walked away across the yard toward the distant line of trees.

9

THEY STRODE ACROSS A MEADOW and when they hit the thicker trees at the edge of it, he dropped into the stalking walk and she followed suit. He moved quickly. She fought with her balance at the forced gait but by the time they crested a small ridge she had the tempo. He led her down the slope and they walked to the edge of a glade that was sheltered by mountains on all sides. There was a small stream and the flat of it was thick with aspen, birch, and willow saplings. He dropped into a crouch behind a fallen pine and peered over the top of it. She moved in beside him and they sat without speaking and watched the sun splay shadows across the tufts of grass and juniper and clutches of wild raspberry. Nothing moved. She breathed as he had taught her and closed her eyes to find the calm within her and when she opened her eyes he was staring at her. He crooked his head toward the far end of the glade. At first she saw nothing but shadow and then a small movement that became a doe stepping gingerly into the lush grasses. The deer raised her head and sniffed at the breeze, and she could see the wet of her nose in the slant of the sun. They were fifty yards away from her. He shifted and sat with his back against the log. She turned and dropped down beside him.

"Touch the deer," he said in a whisper.

"Are you kidding?"

"She's come to graze. Use the trees, the brush. Stalk her."

"She'll bolt."

"Not if you do it right. Be patient. Feel your way to her."

He pointed downwind and she rose to a crouch and moved away from the fallen pine. She kept the deer at her right and skirted through the trees in a wide circle until she had moved behind her and could see the flank of her in the grass. She felt her heart drumming in her chest. There was a wide birch beside her and she slipped into the shadow side of it and leaned against it and tried to calm herself. When her breathing slowed she closed her eyes and breathed through her mouth and felt the arch of the birch at her back and its minute sway in the breeze. She focused on that. The push of the trunk against her back was measured and she found the rhythm of it, and made her breathing slower and deeper until it matched the motion of the tree. She could envision the tree as a whole thing, sense the thinner limbs and branches and the tremor of them, and on up to the poke of the tip in the air, the bend of it more pronounced, and the waft of the breeze against its white and reddish bark. The feel of the tree against her began to disappear. When it did she stepped out into the clear and began to walk toward the doe.

Her breathing grew so shallow she felt as if she were absorbing air through her skin. She put her arms out wide to her side and splayed the fingers of her hands and focused on the deer that stood with its head bent down to the grass, oblivious. There was the rustle of leaves in the breeze. A bird twittered. A mouse twitched about in the dry grass. A garter snake poked its head out from under a flat rock and then wound itself over the lip of it and lay there in the heat of the sun. She stepped past the snake and it didn't move. She could feel the texture of the land against the bottoms of her feet and she rolled each step inward like he'd taught her and allowed the sensations that came to guide the placement of each step. She did not need to look down. Instead, she kept her arms out wide and stepped slowly toward the deer. The distance shrank. The closer she got the more excited she began to feel, and she had to stop and hold her position and calm herself, and breathe and focus on the feel of the land and pull the quiet deep into her and then step again, furtively, gingerly. The doe stepped deeper into the glade, stopping to nibble at willow leaves, and she stepped when it stepped, the stalking so deliberate she felt as though she were levitating above the ground, her outstretched arms like wings.

There was only the light now. Muted. Hushed. Shadow threaded across the breadth of grass. She breathed and reached out for the feel of the light on her skin, silken, tenuous, fragile, and she forced herself into even smaller moves so that it would not shatter. Each step seemed to take minutes. Her body was weightless. She eased forward and the deer kept on grazing, her tail twitching slightly.

She cut to her right. She slip-stepped and approached the doe broadside. She could see all of it now, the tan of it cut by intermittent lines of black and the thrust of its ears, sharp and angled into the breeze. The deer raised her head to get at aspen leaves and Emmy saw the white of its eyes as they rolled toward the shape of the woman at the periphery. She stood there in the opening between saplings and the deer turned its head and studied her. She could see its nostrils working. She stood stock-still and the deer turned back to the aspen and continued to graze. The breeze rose slightly and there was a swishing though the trees, and she used it to step closer until she was a yard from the deer. It turned to look at her and she expected it to bolt but the doe only swivelled its ears to catch the breeze. Her heart drummed again and she stood there for long moments, forcing herself downward into calm, and her breathing slowed and quieted and she slipped a foot through the grass and edged closer to the deer, who looked at her full-on. She reached a hand out into the space between them and it felt airy and unreal, and when she touched the doe with her fingertips she could feel the energy of it against the nub of them and she wanted to scream in exultation. The deer craned its neck up to the leaves again and she put her full palm on its flank and closed her eyes.

She could feel the land at her feet, the breeze on her cheek, and the hot flush of the deer, and she raised her head and felt the sun on her eyelids and wept silently. The deer moved away. She opened her eyes to an empty glade and the feel of the breeze. She turned and he stood there and opened his arms wide, and she stepped into them and let herself cry openly against his chest.

It was late afternoon and the light was shifting. She slumped into the mare's gait and when Starlight kicked the gelding into a trot up the slope, the mare stepped up too, and she caught the shift in gait quickly and leaned up, took the rein in two hands, and rode the trot to the crest, where he slowed the horses down to a walk again. She eased the mare past the spare horse and settled in beside him and they rode the trail side by side.

"When I was a little girl I used to climb inside the cedar chest where my mother kept blankets." The words tumbled out of her almost on their own accord. He rode easily, head down, nodding, listening.

"It was real quiet in there an' it kinda felt like my burrow or somethin'. Like I was a little creature. I'd climb in there and just listen to the silence. Like here. It was like being nowhere and everywhere at the same time. It was magical. I thought I could stay in there forever.

"I was in there the day my ma walked out. They were drunk an' fightin' and yellin' like they always done, an' I heard him slap her an' kick her and her fallin' against the wall an' she left and I never seen her again. Ever. I never went into the chest again after that. I thought if I hadn't been hiding in that chest, all consumed by the silence like that, then maybe I mighta heard something that woulda changed things. Somethin' I coulda said, somethin' I coulda done, somethin' that coulda kept her there. I never forgave her for that. I've been angry ever since. Angry at her for leaving. Angry at him. Angry at all men."

They rode on and Starlight lazed on the horse and she mimicked his posture. The riding was easy. She felt lost but assured in the sway. The scrunch of gravel from the hoofs echoed in the trees.

"I used to fight when I was a kid," he said. "Every day almost. Schoolyard scraps, neighbourhood beefs; hell, I even got into it at Sunday school. They told the old man I was too much of a handful. They said I was wild. But I was just a kid. A kid who never knew where he come from. Who his folks were. Where he belonged. Why he was brown an' the others were white. That's what all the fights were about. Feelin' lost an' not knowin' why. I carried that around a long time an' I never told no one until I told the old man finally. That's when he brung me out here more an' taught me how to touch the deer."

They emerged onto a flat. It was about a quarter-mile wide and he stopped the horses and they sat and looked out across it. He drank from the canteen and handed it to her and she drank and sloshed some into her palm and rubbed it along the back of her neck. The cool of it slick against the heat from the sun.

"We're gonna gallop across that flat," he said.

"But I've never done that."

"Don't mean you can't."

"Might mean I shouldn't."

"We'll take them up to a canter, then give her a squeeze with your legs. She'll take that as you askin' for more. When she breaks into it you'll feel a four-beat kinda thing, *thump thump, thump thump*. Lean into it some but not too much, and kinda move your girdle like you're scooping with it. That way you'll move with her, not against her."

"Easy for you to say."

"Scared?"

"Hell, yeah."

"Good. Ride through it."

He nudged the gelding and they broke out of the trees and he brought the horse to a trot, then a canter. She struggled with the gait. He took them around the clearing so she could get accustomed to the different gait. Then he nudged the gelding up and when it broke she felt the mare respond and tried to remember what he'd told her. She clenched her jaw and leaned forward and tried to discern the rhythm. It took some doing but she found it and they tore across the last two hundred yards and she pushed with her pelvis like he told her and fell into the full force of the gallop. It was a surging feeling unlike anything she'd ever experienced before. The burst of air when all four hoofs cleared the ground. When they stopped she slid off the mare and leaned against the trunk of a tree with her hands on her knees. She was shaking.

He leaned forward on the gelding and crossed his wrists on the pommel. He watched Emmy regain her breath and she huffed out a breath and stood and shook her head and looked up at him. Her face was flushed and her eyes were shimmering with a high excitement.

"My God," she said.

"You touch a deer, you gallop a horse. There's no room in there for hurt or anger. That's where you learn to live when you come to the land."

He nudged the horse again and she remounted and they walked up the slope of the trail. He walked the gelding around the curve of the trail and she let him ride on and climbed down off the mare. She was alone in the trees, the full flush of land around her immense in its push and swell. The western slope was in shadow and she traced the fall of it and closed her eyes, and felt the rush of space and the wild energy of the horse and the thrill in her belly like the great wide open of the sky. She walked to the mare and flung herself aboard. She sat the horse and looked ahead at the trail through the trees. Then she nodded, pulled on the rein, turned the mare to the trail, and nudged her with her heel.

"Git up, girl," she said.

BOOK THREE

UNBROKEN COUNTRY

"THEY REALLY WANT YOU IN VANCOUVER, Frank."
Deacon stared at him intently across the diner table.

Starlight sipped his coffee and gazed out the window at the street. "You know I ain't of a mind to go."

"I know. But I'm thinking of your future. Your career."

"The farm is my career."

"But you're an artist. A singular one, and people want to hear from you, to see you."

"You always said my soul is in them pictures. If that's true, then they don't really need me is what I figure. Besides, me and cities ain't no workin' fit."

Deacon set his cup down on the table and twirled it around slowly. When he looked up at Starlight again his face was intent and grave, and Starlight met his look and they sat in silence while the sound of morning in the small town broke around them. Starlight pursed his lips, took a drink of coffee, and leaned back in the booth seat.

"I know your feelings about that, Frank. But this is a big show at a major gallery, and it would mean so much to your name recognition, not to mention your sales."

"I never got into this for sales."

"I know that too. But your work itself dictated this change. I think you owe it to yourself to show up for this. It doesn't have to be a regular thing. An appearance every now and then. It wouldn't upset your lifestyle or your peace of mind."

"Feels to me like it already has."

"Every great artist compromises for success."

"Gettin' two good crops of hay in a year is success enough for me. When we started this you said you'd take care of all the business stuff. That was our deal."

"I know," Deacon said. "But that was before things took off. Before people began falling in love with your photographs. You're an artist now, Frank. You can't turn the clock back or change what is."

Starlight picked up his cup and drank the rest of the coffee and set the cup down and drummed his fingers on the table. Deacon could see how much the idea of this venture upset him. He waited for the big man to speak.

"Gotta talk to Roth," Starlight said, finally. "I ain't doin' nothin' without Eugene on accounta whatever I choose affects him too. If I go, he has to go with me."

"I'm sure that won't be a problem," Deacon said.

"And Emmy and Winnie. They deserve to see somethin' different. Get away from cow stink and manure for a few days. I'll consider it if you can make all that happen."

"Count on it, Frank."

"No promises. Depends on Roth. I gotta go now. Boards need replacin' on one wall of the barn."

"Okay," Deacon said. "You know, there's not another Native photographer in the country with your acclaim. You're special. Unique. People want to see you."

"Me bein' Indian's got nothin' to do with this. I do what I do because I love it. Old man woulda said that love ain't got no colour or no skin. I pretty much lean to that."

Deacon nodded solemnly. "There's those who will want to put that label on you nonetheless. Native. Photographer. Just so you know that."

"You take the label off a can of beans you still got a can of beans. Seems to me the label don't matter much at all. What counts is what's inside. Another thing the old man said one time."

Deacon smiled. "He was a wise one."

Starlight slid out of the booth and shrugged into his denim jacket and stood looking down at Deacon. He nodded. "He was," he said. "Figure maybe I owe him this trip when it come down to it."

Deacon watched him walk out of the diner and cross the street to the old truck. He filled space easily. Deacon left a fan of bills on the table and rose and made his way to his studio, fascinated all over again by the man he was privileged to call a friend.

The boards they worked to replace were high on the south side of the barn so that labouring on ladders and rope and pulleys with their backs exposed to the hard heat of the sun was draining. Still, they suffered through it. Starlight hauled on the rope to bring the boards up so they could both grab an edge and angle it into place. Roth wore a carpenter's belt and when the board was in place he nailed the top end to the spar that ran the length of that side of the barn. Then they eased down a few rungs. Starlight pressed the board flat to the spar and Roth nailed it again. Each length of lumber took a lot of time to replace. When they were finished they stepped off the ladders and moved into the shade on the north side of the barn, where they sat with their legs splayed and leaned against the cool concrete foundation and drank water from thermoses and wiped at their faces with neckerchiefs then rolled smokes and sat taking long hauls off them without speaking. Starlight leaned his head back against the cool hardness and closed his eyes. He loved the feeling of effort and the satisfaction of work well done. He heard Roth exhale and turned his head and squinted at the skinny man, who grinned at him and nodded.

Roth arched his back and pressed the back of his shoulders against the concrete and sighed. "Well," he said. "Might as well say what ya got to say now before we fix on painting them slabs."

"What makes you think I got somethin' to say?" Starlight asked.

"Like I told ya, Frank. I been around you long enough to know when ya got somethin' in your gut needs gettin' out."

Starlight nodded grimly. "Yeah. Truth is, I do. Spoke to Deacon in town this morning. He thinks I should go to Vancouver for that fancy display of my pictures. Says I owe it to people to be there."

"Whattaya figure?" Roth asked.

"Kinda wanted your take on it before I decide."

"Me? I'm a farm hand. What do I know about your art?"

"Guess I was asking about how you'd feel about comin' with me."

"You want me there, I'm there, pal. But I gotta ask what you're feelin' about it. That's what matters here, not my take on it all."

"You know how I feel about cities."

"Gotta rip 'em off ya like ticks or they'll suck the blood right outta ya. I'm like you in that. Me and cities parted company a long number of years back and I been the better for it since. But this ain't about going to Vancouver is it?"

"No," Starlight said. "Guess it ain't really."

"What is it then? Gotta be big on accounta you don't get all scrunched up about the eyeballs over small stuff. That's pure constipation of thinkin' and carryin' things on your own. Some drink over that. Others act out in all kind of bizarre ways. You? You get more wrinkled up than heifer tits after calving time."

Starlight laughed. "Paint quite a picture, don't ya?"

"I been a spellbindin' word slinger long as I can recall. Cut straight through the fat and gristle right down to the bone's always been my way. You'd be well served to speak like that more often. You'd be less wrinkly that way. So what is it?"

Starlight tapped the steel toes of his work boots together and stared down at the grass. Roth waited him out.

"It's about change, I reckon. A man gets used to the lay of things, the routine. Least I do. I never started this whole picture-takin' thing so that anything would change. It was just the way I always wanted to see the animals and the land. Kinda like freeze 'em in time so they wouldn't never change neither. I never figured on none of this tomfoolery with galleries and talkin' to folks about what's always been a private thing for me. Never figured on makin' no money neither."

"Kinda grew legs didn't it?" Roth asked.

"Yeah. And for the life of me I don't know why."

"Because most folks only got one set of eyes and one way of seein'. You and that camera give 'em a whole other world than what they think they know. Guess in a way that's how come you're here, Frank."

"To be someone's eyeballs?"

"Not so much as showin' them what their own are missin' out on. I know you changed the way I look at things now."

"You talk like what I do is magic."

"It is, chum. It is. You and the land and them creatures are perfect. You go out there and bring back magic Deacon puts in a frame and, pow, you change people, rearrange 'em so they come to understand something more about this world and this life than they ever figured on. That's what an artist does, I figure. And a magician."

"So I should go and talk about magic?"

It was Roth's turn to laugh. "Nah," he said. "I'd go and talk about you. How it feels to be so close to wild animals, nature, the friggin' universe. The pictures will always speak for themselves."

"You'll come with me then?"

"Wasn't never no question about that. 'Sides, the last time I let you even go into Endako on yer own you wound up bringin' home a woman and a kid. Lord knows what you'd haul back here with a whole dang city around you. And I wouldn't be too worried about dealin' with change. You brought on a whole shebang of change that day. And that's the other thing we might as well talk about while we're at it."

"What's that?" Starlight asked.

"You wanting to take Emmy and the girl along."

"How'd you know I was thinking about that?"

"Told ya. You get all scrunched up about the face. You got feelin's you been totin' around inside ya for a while and yer plumb confounded on what to do with them."

"What kinda feelin's you talking about, Eugene?"

"Man-woman feelin's. The both of ya been like cats in heat

strollin' around each other with yer tails in the air, waiting for the other to make the first move. It's in the way ya look at each other when ya think I don't see. All that's missing is the fur flyin' and the yowlin' in the moonlight."

"Yowlin' in the moonlight? What makes you think she's feeling anything for me but grateful?"

"Grateful passed a long time ago, Frank. Ya give her the land. You woke up things she never knew she had in her. Ya showed her that men ain't all like what she grew used to. You taught her that life could be different. Better. Ya showed her how to walk into the possible and ya did it as tender as you treat a green broke colt. Yeah, grateful's way downstream now, pal. And you're carryin' the same ache and don't know what to do about it either."

"I never had a woman. You know that," Starlight said.

"I know. Don't mean ya never had the ache for one."

"She does make me feel awkward, that's for sure. Sometimes there's things I want to say but when it comes to speaking them it's like I never learned how to talk. I feel like I did when I was a kid scratchin' around the dirt with a stick on accounta I never had the words yet."

"Well, if you want to ask her to come to Vancouver ya better put the stick down and talk to her. I think you'll find out that she's been feelin' the same way around you."

"How do you know that for sure?"

"Because, old friend, when it comes to women I'm a walkin', talkin' encyclopedia."

Starlight chuckled. "Then how come in all this time I never ever seen ya with one?"

"Truth?"

"Yeah. Truth."

"I just pure wouldn't want to be responsible for the effect of unleashing all of this raw masculinity on some unsuspecting woman."

Starlight shook his head and stood up and stretched. "Well then, Mr. Masculinity, maybe we better drain some of that off and get them boards painted before the sun goes down and Emmy has supper ready."

Roth clambered to his feet and they gathered the paint cans and brushes and walked to the ladders and climbed and soon lost themselves in the work, grinning at each other from time to time. Roth whistled a jaunty old tune while the sun sank deeper and closer to the serrated teeth of the trees at the edge of the field, and Starlight thought about the old barn and all that it held for him, and how life sometimes is a fresh board you add to something precious and priceless and worth holding on to forever.

She found him standing in the mazy orange lantern glow of the barn, with one foot on the bottom rail of the partition, watching the horses prepare to settle in for the night. She stood beside him with her chin resting on her crossed forearms and admired the sleek calmness of the animals. Starlight glanced at her and when he caught her eye he grinned and nodded. Emmy offered a small smile in return and they stood there drinking in the soft clop of hoofs in the stall and the neighs and whinnies of the horses, the low stink of manure against the fresh chaff of dry straw, and the nutty smell of fresh oats in the trough. The lantern threw flickered shadows against the walls and cobwebbed windows, and Starlight took to studying the beams and rafters while Emmy turned her head and studied him.

"What is it, Frank? Where are you?" she asked.

"I like standing here at the end of a day," he said. "This old barn holds a lot of me and I guess when I feel unsettled it feels better here than anywhere except maybe the land."

"I find it charming," Emmy said.

"Whattaya mean?"

"You never changed anything. You kept it the same all these years except for the fixups and repainting that needed doing. But I walk in here and I can almost feel the years."

"I kept the old man here a long time after he died. His ashes, I mean. Kept his urn on a shelf in the tack room on accounta I didn't know where he'da wanted them spread. Took me a couple years to figure that out. But sometimes it's like I can feel him beside me in here. Comforting. You know?"

"Not really. But I can imagine it. I never had a special place all my life. Not until I came here anyway."

Starlight turned to face her and leaned against the partition with one arm. "Funny thing is, the place I settled on wasn't even here or anywhere on the property."

"Where was it then?"

"Someplace the old man never even been. Two days' ride from here. In the backcountry, where no one ever goes. Not even the quads and motorbikes. Pure horse country. I found it one day and it dawned on me that it was the spot where he'd be at peace."

"What made you think that?"

"Never a footprint there except mine, the horses, and the wild things. No sign or scar of man anywhere," Starlight said. "Them kinda places are gettin' more and more scarce every year but ya can still find 'em if you look hard enough and you wanna be there strong enough.

"So I took him there. Sat on a ridge facing west and when the sun threw the sky into shades of red and orange I never seen before either, I flung his ashes into the breeze and let him settle over all that beauty. Kinda felt him right there beside me when I done that and I knew I chose right.

"Unbroken country. It was where he come to find himself when he was still nimble enough to ride. He give the love of it to me. I go to that ridge now and again and I always come back more peaceful, settled, anchored. Guess it turned out in the end that it was the reason I wasn't meant to leave here."

Emmy's face was soft in the flicker of the lantern. "That's beautiful. Unbroken country. I don't know as I've ever seen it. Or if I did I never recognized it for what it was."

"I figure it lives in a soft spot in the heart," Starlight said and turned to face the horses again.

"There's so much to you, Frank. So many layers. I'm always grateful when you share them with me."

"People are unbroken country too," he said.

"What do you mean?"

"Guess I mean that when you walk into one of them places for the first time ya feel spooked kinda, scared, not sure of what you'll find there or if ya can find your way out once you're in. Like coming to know someone. Losing yourself in what ya find."

She stood and turned to face him directly and when he noticed he turned to her as well. They stood looking at each other and the horses neighed quietly and there was the sound of a night owl high in the rafters then a hushed flutter of wings, and the barn lapsed into silence again.

"I feel like I'm in unbroken country here, Frank," Emmy

said. "I didn't want to speak of it. Scared, I guess, that if I said anything I'd lose what I was finding."

"And what is it you're finding?" Starlight asked.

"Something I never had before. Something Winnie never had either. A place where we feel safe, secure. Where I don't have to keep a candle burning in the dark so I can sleep. A home, I guess. But it's you too. I'm finding you and I don't want to lose that.

"My life ain't perfect. Never has been. There's been a lot of men. A lot of pain and struggle. All kinds of hopes and dreams dashed and smashed and broken. All kinds of do-overs that never worked out, and I come away from all of it feeling and believing that I deserved nothing different. That my life was supposed to be one long unhealed bruise.

"Here, with you, it's different. Like time moves different. Like I move different. Like there's something drawing me forward deeper into this country that I don't recognize."

Starlight stretched his arms open wide and Emmy stepped close to him shyly. He pulled her close to his chest and brushed her hair back along her temple gently with the tips of his fingers. "Ya know the smallest mare? The one Winnie rides?" he asked her.

"Yeah. She loves that horse."

"Well, she come here from the animal rescue. Fella that had her didn't tend to her or any of his other stock. They were all sick and dehydrated, starving, beaten, skittish as all hell. She was the worst of the lot. She wouldn't even let me close for the longest time. Had to keep her in a pen by herself on accounta she was fearful of the other horses."

"But she's so gentle now. So calm and settled," Emmy said.

"I'd come out here and roll up in a blanket and sleep the night with her. Never make a sudden move or try to get closer. Took weeks but she come to trust me and soon I could feed her oats outta my hand. She let me brush her out and I'd walk her by the halter around the pasture on accounta all the hurt made her forget how to be a horse. I'd walk her every day. Then I'd trot, then full-out run, and pretty soon when she got her strength back I could turn her loose in that field and she'd gallop and play like the horse she was meant to be. Didn't try to change her at all. Just let her find herself in the love I was giving.

"So I guess I figure that love's unbroken country too. Me an' that little mare moved into it together and she became a really good horse. It didn't make all the hurt she felt before disappear. Didn't change anything that come before. It just made her able to forget it and live a different way. The way she was meant to.

"Having you here's like that for me," Starlight said. "You make me forget how I lived up to now. And if it helps at all, I'm scared too. Scared to speak of it, of ruining it, changing it into something else, and losing it. Was Roth give me enough gumption to let you know where I was with things."

Emmy stepped back from him a half-step. "Well, here's to Eugene," she said.

She stood on her tiptoes and reached up and pulled his face down and kissed him softly. The gentle warmth took Starlight by surprise and he kissed her back, taking care to be tender, calm, unhurried through the pounding of his heart. He leaned forward so she could move off her tiptoes. She opened her mouth and the feel of her tongue on his was an elegant frenzy and he pulled her to him, careful not to break the embrace. He let his tongue move in unison with hers and the effect was dizzying, and he wanted to moan but held his silence and let the kiss take on its own rhythm. He felt stirrings strange and unfamiliar moving in him and he let himself feel them, and when she finally broke the kiss and stepped back to look at him he grinned shyly.

"What was that for?" he asked.

"For unbroken country," she said.

Then she kissed him again.

2

THEY DROVE AND LINGERED DAYS IN Field and Trail
and Castlegar, the small mountain towns where lumbermen
lived and worked, but wending their way through that endless
beauty brought nothing to Cadotte but a heavier, harder spear
of rage and he took no comfort in drink or women or the feigned
comradery and quick friendships spawned by big money, sweat,
and lives lived untethered and wild. Instead, he took to fight-
ing. He found that he could lose himself in savagery. That thick
coil of vengeance he carried in his gut could unsnake itself and
take on the qualities of fists and kicks and hammer blows to
heads and bellies and the cracking and breaking of teeth and ribs
and other bones. So that he found a grim satisfaction in pushing
men to fight. In those booze-filled nights in working men's
towns, such contests of will and rage were easy to start and he
let the vehemence of his shattered ego rain punishment on men
in ones or twos or threes. He was thrilling to watch. For such
a bulky man he was light on his feet and lizard fast. He pun-
ished men. He knew precisely how hard and often to attack
and hit, and he toyed with them, bloodying faces and battering
knees and hips and shoulders so that in the end his adversar-
ies became limp, defenceless rags of men who dropped at his

feet eventually, and he'd raise his fists and face to the ceiling of the sky and howl in a basso keening imbued with every ounce of hate he carried for the woman he hunted unceasingly. She would be his ultimate triumph. Besting men was only the venting outlet for his vitriol and he sought and found it everywhere.

For his part, Anderson watched and pondered as deeply as he was capable the fury Cadotte could unleash. He'd rub at his own scars and feel the clutch of resentment and anger. But it paled in comparison. Cadotte simmered in a rich venomous stew and there was a part of Anderson that understood and feared it at the same time. He couldn't harm a child. He knew that. After all those months on the road he wasn't even certain he could hurt Emmy. The unrelenting prowling through bars and low neighbourhoods had tired him, made him sad almost at the lot so many people drew, and he looked back at his own meagre upbringing and the ruptured family life that booze and drugs and chronic poverty had caused and wished secretly for a way to simply walk away from Cadotte's stalking journey. They might not find them anyway. It was a big country and Emmy was cagey enough to know where to go to ground for safety and anonymity. He knew that now. So while Cadotte raged, Anderson brooded and watched for his chance to alter his own course.

But Cadotte was a black hole that absorbed and killed everything, and made it disappear into a whirling vortex whose only gravity was pain. Still, Anderson wondered if there was a way of escaping the heavy pull of all that sullen energy.

He was at the wheel as they drove through the harrowing curves of road that dipped severely from the heights of cordillera to the flat, semi-desert of Grand Forks and Osoyoos. It was wonderful territory but he was too fraught with anxiety to appreciate it. He didn't fear Cadotte. But any word that went against his intention was liable to throw him into a fury that only fists and boots could resolve. Anderson didn't need the taste of his own blood in his mouth so he spoke his mind carefully now.

"You worry me, Jeff," he said.

"Worry you how exactly?" Cadotte answered. He slouched in his seat with a soiled and tattered John Deere hat pulled low over his eyes.

"Yer wild and gettin' wilder."

"Sowing oats is all I'm doing."

"No. Ya moved past that three towns ago. Now you're downright vicious."

"I never been the polite type."

"I know that. But that guy last night? Ya coulda stopped at the broken nose. But ya pulled him to his feet and knocked his teeth out. Then you threw him out the door and over the railing into the parking lot."

"Fuckin' guy bit me," Cadotte said and held up the knuckles of his right hand. The bite mark was evident.

"By then it was all he could do. You had him. He was done but you just kept on plowing into him. Yer lucky the owner didn't call the cops."

"Yeah, well, I guess God give some people enough sense to go on livin' didn't he."

"But he coulda. Then what kinda shape would we be in? I don't favour lockup. I'm too damn old for that shit."

"At least I'm out there swingin'. I don't recall seein' you jump in when someone's buddies come for backup."

"You don't need my help. You're a madman."

"I got her harnessed."

"It don't look it. Makes me wonder if yer gonna be careful enough not to leave sign even if we do find Emmy."

"Oh, we'll find her. And I ain't crazy enough to leave anything that points to us. Believe me."

"Still worries me."

"Let it. I don't give a shit."

"That worries me too."

"Why?"

"Because we're talkin' major charges and major time if we let anything lead back to us. You ain't out fer evening things up, Jeff. You're out for revenge. Big-time."

"So you think I ain't capable? That I'm wacko? Looney tunes?"

"No. I ain't sayin' that. What I'm sayin' is I think ya gotta ease back on the throttle some is all."

"Don't get yer panties in a knot. I know what I'm doing."

"Then tell me what that is so I know too."

"I'm openin' the valve and lettin' off steam so's I can think straight when the time comes."

"That's one hell of a lot of steam yer carryin' then."

Cadotte sat straight up and pushed the cap back on his head and turned to face Anderson, who glanced quickly at him and then back at the road. "You had the same stoked up when we started this. Makes me kinda wonder about you now too."

"I'm still here ain't I?"

"Are ya? Really? Or you just puttin' in time to make a good show of yerself so I don't pound into you too?"

Anderson turned his head and glared at Cadotte. "I told ya, Jeff. I don't fear you. You can bring shit anytime so long as ya can take it back when it's handed out."

Cadotte laughed mockingly. "If that time were ever to come, Anderson, you'd be wishin' ya had yer mama to hide behind. Trust me."

"I'm tryin' to trust you, Jeff. But you're makin' it hard by the way yer actin'. And don't worry about me. I ain't left the bus."

"That's good because this bus is goin' all the way to the end of the road. And findin' Emmy? My gut's leadin' me and I can tell ya we're gettin' close. Ain't nothing to stop us now but someone backin' off and that ain't likely to be me."

"Me neither. Just so ya know."

"That's good. Any more frettin' ya wanna talk out or you done wimperin'?"

"No wimpering from me. I was just choosing to speak my mind is all. Clear the air, ya know?"

Cadotte was silent. "Ain't no clearin' of no air gonna happen until Emmy gets what's due. You'n me? We look in the fucking mirror every day, see them scars she left, remember how it felt crawlin' out of that blazin' wreck of a cabin and the fuckin' pain of it. Remember she tried to kill us. Can you still do that?"

They drove out of a long, snaking curve and onto a small plateau and they could see the land spread out before them shimmering in the heat and distance below them. Anderson found himself wishing for a calm place like that beyond all roads and thoughts of vengeance, and wondered if he could ever come to that, break free of Cadotte's hold on him and leave, wander off alone to find the shelter of another cabin on a verdant green plain on the side of a river, smoking a pipe on a porch and growing old quietly, easily, without the jut of anger, resentment, and unspoken fear pressing against the inside of his ribs. He glanced at Cadotte, who stared out the windshield too. He wondered where his thoughts took him. But all he could sense was a horrible cloud of darkness around the man and he felt anxious and overwhelmed.

"I can still do that," he said finally and drove down onto that shimmering plain with a river running through it and wondered if it was true.

3

STARLIGHT TOOK THE ROPE HACKAMORE from its peg in the tack room and put it on the old mare and rode her bareback up the ridge beyond the field in the first gauzy light of morning. They were set to leave in a rented car later that day and he wanted to spend time alone on the land to ground himself for the jangle of the city. The horse was happy with the walk and she neighed and tossed her head, and Starlight smiled at the familiar gaiety and small jounce to her step. They made the top of the ridge just as the sun flooded the valley below in a scarlet flush leaning to orange, and he dismounted and walked to a large rock and sat while the horse was content to nibble at twitch grass. He liked the small echo the clop of her hoofs cast back at him from across that verdant depth of space below. He rolled a smoke and sat eyeing the horizon to the southwest. From the farm, the land would slowly begin to fall away, descending gradually then sharply to the coast and the strait and the sea he'd only seen once before. The route he'd chosen to drive would give Emmy and the girl an opportunity to experience vistas that would fill them with the same joy he felt watching the land assert itself, become itself, and he smiled knowing the look of wonder that would set upon their faces as they travelled through it all.

He wanted that for them. Emmy had agreed to go readily. They'd packed the night before and he and Roth had loaded the trunk with suitcases and packs before they'd retired to their beds. Now, sitting in solitude, studying the wide expanse of peak and plain and snowcap, he moved out of anxiety and welcomed the adventure the city and the showing at the gallery would bring. That surprised him. He had no truck with hustle and bustle nor the radical palette of colour and light and noise the city offered and had gone out of his way for years in order to avoid it. But that kiss in the barn lingered on his lips and he found himself wanting to bring Emmy and Winnie to the world and the world to them even if he didn't crave much of it beyond the farm himself. He touched his lips lightly with one finger. It had simply been a mouth before. Now, it was altered as he was altered by the mystery of a woman, her touch, her warmth, the secret promise in that embrace that drew him deeper, further into its hold.

He'd tried to track the trail that had led to that moment in the barn but all signs eluded him. Instead, it sat in him as a sudden surprise, shocking, like that instant when the flicker of lantern light throws the hard yellow eyes of an owl in the rafters into a phosphorescent glow staring right into the inner depths of a man. He'd liked the heady feeling of being totally, witlessly, out of control. He thought of the smallness of her feet, the balmy span of her hand on his shoulders and neck and cheek. The undiscovered map of his being was granted an extra dimension and he grinned and tapped his feet like a young boy dancing in a corn field. The horse whinnied at his sally and brought him back into focus.

There was birdsong now and the bawl of cattle in the free range and Starlight knew it as the backdrop of his whole life.

He drank in the morning sounds and when he felt filled he stood and stretched and ambled to the horse, mounted, and walked her to the edge of the face of the ridge. He surveyed it all again before turning and riding back down the trail to the farm, where life and mystery and possibility waited for him to claim it. When the cover of the trees broke and the farm spread out before him he knew what he would say to the people at the gallery. Home. How a man can come to find it on the land, in the creatures it held, in the bowl of the sky easing down over it, and how that same man might capture it forever in a photograph or paint or words so others who might never get the chance might clutch it to their chests and be filled as he was filled by the land. He grinned and kicked the old mare up to a trot and readied himself for the journey.

Emmy rode in the front seat beside Starlight, and Roth and Winnie sat in the back. They plowed through the high plateau of the Cariboo and south at Prince George through Quesnel and Williams Lake, and Emmy felt her belly clutch at the familiar territory of their flight. The farms and ranches were charming. Winnie laughed and joked and teased with Roth. Neither Starlight nor Emmy spoke much, both of them content to watch the land change around them. When they entered the arid, semi-desert near Cache Creek and swung left toward Lillooet, none of them could speak. The land held them in its hypnotic sway as they rounded sweeping curves at the edges of sheer gaping plummets to a river reduced to a thin blue churn far below them. They climbed vertiginous cliffs and ridges where it seemed the face of rock would push them off the asphalt and the views

were spellbinding in their panoramic grandeur. Sudden patches
of open ground held huge bushes of sage. Mountain sheep lifted
their heads as they passed. Now and then they saw what might
have been wild mustangs charging across clearings and the effect
was that of time displaced and the sensation of witnessing what
once was before man and settlement altered it forever.

Starlight took his time driving through it. He pulled over often
so they could stand in the energy of that sere, rocky land. He had
his camera and he took pictures of Emmy and Winnie on a look-
out above a steep canyon and beyond to the flank of mountain
and the endless azure of the sky so that it seemed they were
pinned to it, the mountains setting a jagged frame to their beings.
Winnie gathered a small bunch of sage and Roth tied it together
with string. She held it to her nose and inhaled its pungent tang
then ran and offered it to Emmy, who did the same, and when
she looked up at Starlight her eyes were aflame with excitement. They all turned then and marvelled at the intensity of that
impeccable, irreproachable space. Emmy eased closer and put
her hand to Starlight's back and he offered a shy grin and she
smiled. When they'd had enough they climbed back into the
car. The ravines and gullies and promontories a seeming arm's
length away lulled them all into silence and the drive became a
hushed communion with everything, and the morning was
swept away with that quiet act of ceremony and the sanctified
air of the sage Winnie asked to be tied to the rear-view mirror.

"It's like a dream," Winnie said quietly.

Later, they sat on the shore of a lake caught between two
towering mountains and ate the lunch Emmy had packed. Then
Starlight napped while Emmy, Roth, and Winnie explored the
shore and gathered rocks and skipped them across the becalmed

surface of the lake. When he woke, Emmy agreed to drive and they continued on into land that was more verdant, and the highway became a meandering calm with copses of aspen and poplar and oak. They made Pemberton and stopped to watch horses run across broad pastures and to admire the elongated lushness of the valley there. The road changed again to humps and hills, and the mountains were so towering that they were rendered speechless again as they passed Whistler and Squamish, where the strait ran alongside the highway and they were lost in the diamond sparkle of the water and the ancient, briny smell wafting in off the water through the half-opened windows of the car.

Vancouver when they entered it was a shining city by the sea. The late-afternoon sun made all the white, beige, and pale pink buildings appear to shimmer and the glass of the downtown towers held mirrored fragments of the nearby mountains and the sparkle of the strait beyond the long, wide harbour. The traffic grew thick and heavy and fast, and Emmy was unnerved by the speed of it.

"Pull 'er over," Roth said. "Ain't been a road made I can't navigate. Regular stock car, pedal-to-the-metal type when it comes to drivin', me."

They followed road signs that took them over a long suspension bridge and on into the mayhem of the downtown core. Roth was relaxed at the wheel and Starlight called out directions to him and they found the hotel easily. It was impressive. They entered a circular covered driveway that was filled with hundreds of amber lightbulbs, and uniformed valets took the car to park it and put their luggage on a cart and led them to

the front desk, where Starlight introduced himself. The keys
were ready and there was an envelope for Starlight from Deacon
and they followed the valet to the elevator. Winnie stared
around her wide-eyed, reaching out to touch furnishings, wallpaper, and the deep lush carpeting.

"It's like being in *Cinderella*," she said.

Their rooms were side by side and Starlight and Roth could
hear squeals of excitement when they stood at the window of
their room, staring out across the jutted angles of the city. The
envelope held a letter with directions to the gallery and infor-
mation about restaurants Deacon favoured and things to do to
fill up their evening. Starlight and Roth took turns showering
and changing and when they were finished Starlight phoned
Deacon while Roth catnapped on one of the two king-size
beds. There was a knock on the adjoining door and Starlight
opened it and Winnie ran in and gazed out the window. Emmy
entered demurely and put a hand on Starlight's chest and he
looked at her and smiled. When Roth stirred they made a decision to walk and find a place to take their evening meal.

The streets were awhir with people and the noise was hard
and harsh to their ears. But Winnie was fascinated by everything and she held Roth's hand and tugged him along from
storefront to storefront. Emmy took Starlight's hand and he
walked awkwardly at first then found the grace of it and they
ambled slowly behind Roth and Winnie.

"Thank you," Emmy said.

Starlight could find no answer so he just grinned, squeezed
her hand, and pointed to things that caught his eye. They
walked all the way to Stanley Park and Winnie fed birds from
a bag of popcorn Starlight got her and when their hunger

finally hit they made their way to a restaurant Deacon recommended. It sat in a cleared space rimmed with trees and a lush carpet of lawn that provided a view of the strait. The food was fabulous and when they were done, it was full evening and they walked the streets until tiredness hit and they walked back to the hotel. Roth and Winnie lay on one of the beds and flipped through channels on the television. Emmy and Starlight stood at the window, gazing at the multitude of lights.

"This was an amazing day, Frank. Winnie is so thrilled. I can't thank you enough for this," Emmy said.

"Can't thank you enough for makin' the trip with us," Starlight said.

"I wouldn't have missed it for the world."

"Me neither now I'm here. Took some doin'."

"It's worth the wranglin'."

"Still ain't no big fan of it. The city, I mean."

"We don't have to be. We can just enjoy it while we're here."

"I can do that."

"I know you can. Are you nervous about tomorrow?"

"Not so much. Sittin' on the ridge this mornin' put me in a good spot with it."

"You'll do great. Just look at me and tell me what you want to say."

"I like the idea of that."

She smiled. "I like the idea of you liking it."

He laughed.

They turned to look at Roth and Winnie. The girl was nestled against the skinny man and fast asleep with her head against his ribs. He had an arm draped protectively around her. When he caught their gaze he grinned and nodded, and Emmy put a hand to her throat and choked back a moan.

"You men are so special," she said.

"Well, you and Winnie are mighty special yourselves."

"We should get her into her own bed."

Starlight crossed the room to where Roth lay and held out his hands and took the girl and lifted her out of Roth's grasp. Roth stood and held out his own hands to take Winnie back and walked to the adjoining door then turned and winked at the two of them.

"I'll tuck her in," he said. "You two say your good nights."

He disappeared into the next room.

Emmy and Starlight stood there uncertain of what to do or say. Finally, Emmy stepped close and wrapped her arms around him and held him tightly. Starlight lay his chin on the top of her head.

"Frank," was all she could find to say.

"Emmy," Starlight said.

He felt like he understood what that meant to him.

4

THE GALLERY OCCUPIED THE CORNER of two busy streets seemingly dedicated to shops run by artists, artisans, and crafters interspersed with swank boutiques and upscale furniture stores, jewellers, and tourist shops. People seemed to radiate wealth and good taste and Starlight felt himself growing anxious at the idea of standing in front of a crowd of the well-heeled and gentrified. Emmy had insisted he buy a white shirt and he was awestruck at the price of things and uncomfortable in the rich cotton feel of the shirt. The gallery itself was constructed of floor-to-ceiling glass windows and lit by rows of track lighting that threw hard white light everywhere and erased shadow completely. He felt laid bare by it. His photographs were arranged on the walls and on pyramidal stands placed strategically around the main room to encourage inspection. He'd never seen so many of his photos on display together and it amazed him that he'd captured so much. The room was abuzz with conversation and when he entered heads swivelled to regard him. He felt the effect of his bulk and put his head down and walked shyly to the rows of chairs set up in front of an oaken podium with twin microphones aimed at its centre. He removed his jacket and hung it on the back of one of the chairs in the front row and Roth,

Emmy, and Winnie followed suit. Then Emmy took him by the hand and walked him to a small bar where a bartender in a crisp white shirt and black vest served them iced water that Starlight drank off in three huge gulps. He stood staring at the empty glass, twirling the ice in it slowly in his hand. Emmy stood beside him while Roth and Winnie inspected the array of photographs.

"They're wonderful, Frank," Emmy said.

"Never seen 'em all at one time," Starlight said. "Kinda weird given I know the when and where of each of 'em. It's like a tour of my life."

He heard his name shouted and turned to see Deacon hustling across the room toward them.

"It's a smash, Frank," Deacon said. "We have upwards of a hundred and twenty people, art reviewers from three major newspapers, and some high-profile buyers and collectors. They're all anxious to hear from you."

"I never knew I done so many," Starlight said.

"Well, the truth is that the earlier work was sold before I gleaned how important a photographer you would really become. There's a lot out there in private hands not represented here. I have the negatives, but I didn't process them for this showing."

"That's what this is called? A showing?"

"Yes. It's what every artist hopes for."

"I'm wishin' for my milkin' pail and my back porch really."

Deacon laughed and put a hand on the big man's shoulder. "You'll do fine. They already love you."

"Don't even know me."

"They get the feeling that they do from the effect of your work. That's why there's so many people here. They want to be near the man who caught such intimate moments forever."

"Hope I can do 'em justice."

"You will," Deacon said. "I'll wait a few minutes and then introduce you and we're off to the races."

Starlight nodded and he and Emmy walked slowly among the photographs, stopping to shake hands and exchange pleasantries with people who hailed him. He felt less discomfited with Emmy at his side. She'd splurged on a good dress and shoes and had taken great care in applying makeup so that she seemed to radiate and Starlight felt pride standing with her in the bustle and noise of that room. When they heard Deacon's voice over the microphone they made their way to their seats and Winnie hugged him tightly. Roth grinned and nodded.

Deacon's introduction was brief and when he stood and made his way to the podium Starlight was surprised at the level of applause at the mention of his name. He stood back from the podium and heaved a great breath and took a sip of water from a glass set on a small table to the side of the podium. Then he stepped up to it and eyed the crowd. They were polished and shiny faces and they were all angled up to look at him. He didn't see any he could attribute to being Indian. These people seemed to be from various backgrounds and the common connection was apparently good fortune and wealth. He rubbed at the thighs of his jeans then placed his hands on either side of the podium and cleared his throat. He looked straight at Emmy and she offered a small grin and nodded. He took one final breath, began to speak, and time disappeared.

"I ain't one to know what it is you want to hear about what I do. It surprises the heck outta me that so many of ya would come to see all this and it surprises me a great deal more that you'd part with cash in order to take some home. I never started taking pictures with any of that or this in mind at all. If anything, I started so's I could fill a big chunk of lonesome I felt at my centre a few years back now. I was suddenly alone on a farm in the mountains where I been all my life an' I got the notion to start takin' a camera with me on my long outings on the land.

"I been doin' that all my life. I take a horse and a few things I need to pitch a camp and head out alone into that open country. Now there's some would call that lonesome but I never found that there. Instead, right from when I was a boy, I felt it fill me. I never felt I needed nothin' in order to cope, handle it, find my way in it. The old man who raised me, and whose passin' created that big lonesome that's responsible for all these pictures bein' taken, had me out on the land on horseback from the moment I can first remember. It was my playground in the beginnin' and then it was my school and finally it become my home on accounta the love of that old man. That open country is so huge you can feel lost and abandoned in it or you can work to feel a part of it, like ya belong to it and it belongs to you. Like a part of you is rock and stone and stream and all the open sky. Ya get past lonesome then and that's how I come to feel after the old man died an' I suppose I started takin' pictures because them creatures is all my family and I'm family to them as well. Folks walk around with family pictures in their wallets nowadays. I wanted to hang mine on walls. Everyone needs family around. That big chunk of lonesome crumbled off with the first photo I took, and it was Deacon there who developed my first rolls of film and said there was something special to them.

"I never understood that. I never knew what to do with them words at all. See, a man can't track an animal unless he comes to know somethin' of that animal itself. The way it works out in the open country is that when ya come to know the way of a bear say, ya come to know somethin' of the whole world and somethin' of yourself all at the same time. Ya learn more of the bear's way and the trackin's easy 'cause yer mostly followin' yourself. That's how I come to get so close to them. There ain't no threat in me. No fear. I'm letting myself live in that big country an' that big country comes to live inside of me. Them creatures sense that. The old man told me one time, he said, 'Frank, never forget that we're animals too.' I ain't never forgot that. It's behavn' like an animal, like a creature, that allows me to get so close to 'em on accounta they recognize one of their own.

"Some say that I can do what I do on accounta I'm Indian. But I wasn't raised Indian. I don't know that I know what I was raised as. The old man had no truck with churches or religions of any sort. He mostly had no proper teachin'. He only ever had the land and that's what he gave to me. I figure I can do what I do because that land's my home. That land's my deepest wish, my wildest dream, the only prayer and the only temple I'm ever gonna need.

"There's great love out there. I know that better'n most because it was the land that was my mother all my life and it always will be. That might sound Indian. I don't know. All's I know is that it sounds like me. My truth. What I carry around inside my belly now instead of lonesome. Lately, I'm comin' to know more of love and I sorta think it ain't no great mystery at all when ya look for the core of it, an' that core is that lovin' something or someone is you allowing it or them to lead ya back to who you really are.

"Them creatures sense that I know that and they let me shoot them as they really are. Ain't no big secret. Like everythin' else in this life it all comes back to love. I'm not askin' them to pose or rearrange or alter themselves a whit to please me. Just let me capture a tiny bit of who they really are. An' the payoff ain't in big fancy shows like this. The payoff is in knowing that I'm capturing a bit of who I really am at the same time.

"Love is unbroken country. Every step ya take deeper into it changes you. Makes you more. Changes the geography of who ya are. And if yer brave enough to enter it alone and find your place in it, ya can't never be lonesome again on accounta you come to live in everything love touches. I only hope every picture I take shows I'm still believin' that."

He walked to his seat and the applause was thunderous around him. Emmy stood and hugged him, her eyes glistening with tears. Roth stood too and shook his hand wholeheartedly, and when he sat Winnie came and sat in his lap and wrapped her arms around his neck and squeezed hard. He laid his hands on her small back and felt the warmth of her spread across his palms. Deacon thanked him and announced that Starlight would sign purchases at a table set up against the wall behind the podium. People rose and moved back into the show area and there was a great hubbub of talk and appreciation for the works on display. It seemed to Starlight that the line for signatures would never end and he scanned the room for Emmy, Roth, and the girl. When the crowd finally dwindled and the gallery room began to clear he stood with Deacon at the bar while Deacon sipped wine and he drank more water for his parched throat. He had a brief conversation with the newspaperman Deacon had told him about and when the reporter left Starlight rejoined Emmy and they prepared to leave.

"You did amazingly well, Frank," Deacon said. "For someone afraid to speak to people you didn't give a hint of that."

"Yeah, well, the podium kept 'em from seein' my knees knockin' together," Starlight said.

"It was a beautiful speech, Frank," Emmy said.

"You looked bigger up there," Winnie said.

"Geez," Roth exclaimed. "This galoot gets to be any bigger we're gonna have to build a bigger house."

They all laughed and Deacon shook Starlight's hand and they made ready to walk back to the hotel.

"That story will be in tomorrow's paper, Frank. I'll bring you back a copy. And again, thanks for doing this. I know how much it took for you to do it," Deacon said.

"Don't know where all them words come from but they appeared to like it."

"They were hanging on your every word, my friend. You did well."

They shook hands again and the four of them walked out of the gallery and into the street, where there was still a lot of foot traffic and Starlight was amazed at the sheer numbers, all framed in a backdrop of neon and storefront.

"I'm gonna get this young'un back to the room and into bed," Roth said. "Then I'm gonna lay out and see if I can find a movie on any of them hundred or so channels. You two take your time gettin' back. I got this," Roth said.

"Thanks, Eugene," Emmy said and hugged him.

"Now that there's prime babysittin' fees. My pleasure," he said. "I'll see ya both later."

They watched Roth and Winnie head back in the direction of the hotel. Starlight breathed deeply of the night air and when he was ready he nodded and they walked down the street together in silence. Emmy took his hand but he slung his arm about her shoulders and they moved together through the great bustle of the city night. They crossed at an intersection and Starlight stopped to look at a display of wood carvings and Emmy reached up and gently touched his cheek and turned his face toward her and stood on her tiptoes to kiss him. The kiss lingered a long time while people flowed past, and when he broke it off and opened his eyes and looked at her he could find no words so he settled for putting a hand to her waist and they moved together toward the hotel.

Neither of them saw the two hulking men following slowly behind them.

5

"I TOLD YOU WE'D TRACK HER DOWN," Cadotte said.

They sat in a dingy bar with a sad country song in the background and the noise of people seeking to lose themselves in booze, the night, and perhaps the company of a random stranger.

A Note on the Ending

Richard Wagamese died on March 10, 2017, before he was able
to complete a draft of this novel. Based on the recollections of
trusted intimates with whom Richard periodically shared his
ideas about his novel-in-progress, we have some indication of
what he intended for the remainder of the book.

There was to be a tender love scene between Frank and
Emmy, which shows Frank, a man who has lived without a
female figure in his life, learning how to relate to a woman, and
Emmy, a woman who has been abused throughout her life,
learning how to trust a man. Their burgeoning love changes
them both in profound ways.

When Frank, Emmy, Roth, and Winnie leave Vancouver and
return to the farm, Cadotte and Anderson follow them. Once
they make their presence known, Cadotte and Anderson are
lured into the backcountry around Frank's farm, where they
are tracked by Frank or Emmy, or both. Eventually, the men
are restrained. Then Emmy, now armed with a knife, aggres-
sively confronts Cadotte and Anderson—and struggles with
her long-simmering rage and desire for revenge against the men
who have hurt her. Richard, however, believed that "despite
everything, every horror, it is possible to move forward and to

learn how to leave hurt behind."* The arcs of his novels tend toward reconciliation and healing, and *Starlight* was to be no different. Frank's gentle influence guides Emmy to the realization that violence will not bring her peace, and in the end she shows Cadotte and Anderson mercy.

In 2007, Richard Wagamese wrote a collection of three novellas. Although the collection was never published, he later expanded two of the novellas into his novels *Indian Horse* and *Medicine Walk*. The third novella, titled "To Fight No More Forever," provides the foundation for *Starlight*, and several of the scenes set in the backcountry around Frank's farm are taken directly from the novella. There are clues that Richard intended to adapt the last scene of "To Fight No More Forever" for the final scene of this novel (we know, for instance, that Richard intended the last line of *Starlight* to be "And then they began to run"). We present the novella's concluding scene here as an epilogue, so readers might have an idea of what Richard envisioned for *Starlight*'s closing pages.

---

* From the essay "Returning to Harmony" by Richard Wagamese.

THEY RAN EASILY THROUGH THE TREES. There were seven of them and they loped across the alpine meadow where it broke open before them and a few of them nipped playfully at the back paws of the ones in front. When they hit the trees on the other side they changed speed and ran lower to the ground, more purposeful, and silent. There was no playfulness. Instead, the wolves prowled and their muzzles were pressed close to the ground, and the alpha wolf steered them steadily forward, only altering course to avoid a thicket or clump of boulders. They ran relentlessly. At the top of a rise they broke into a lope and against the skyline they were shadow runners, skimming across the line of earth and sky, the bounding rise and fall of them a great wild and kinetic wave, and the man and the girl loped behind them and followed them into the trees on the downward side of the rise. The wolves snaked down the cut and when they reached the bottom where a stream flowed, they stopped and huddled on the huge rocks strewn about the shore. The man and the girl trotted out of the trees and waded across the stream a hundred yards from the pack and made their way down the opposite shore until they were directly across from them. The alpha wolf watched them and when they settled down on their haunches among the rocks, he lay down and panted and then rested his muzzle on his forepaws.

The girl stood. She crept forward, easing over the rocks until she climbed atop a large flat stone and knelt there, keeping her eyes on the alpha male. They stared at each other across the brief width of stream. The great wolf sat up. The others followed suit. In the silvered purple light of the moon they gathered around the alpha male and stared across at the girl. She slid the camera from her back and raised it and aimed at the pack, who sat like triangular shadows with only the glint of their eyes visible. She pulled the focus tight and the wolves seemed to stare right into the lens, intent and wild, perched mere yards away, facing the girl and the camera. When the whir of the shutter sounded they stood as one and with a look over his shoulder the leader trotted from the rock and leapt forward into the trees and she could see the line of them ease into the shadows of the trees and disappear. Only then did she breathe. She clambered off the rock and the man stood, waiting by the water. He bent forward on his knees and scooped water in his palm and drank and she did the same. He stood and motioned to the trees with his chin. The girl slung the camera back around onto the flat of her back. She looked at him. He smiled at her in the moonlight. Then she stepped toward the trees and broke into a crouching run and the man watched her disappear silently into the shadow. He smiled again. Then he ran after her.

Publisher's Note

When Richard Wagamese died, we lost one of our most beloved and important storytellers. And so when Richard's literary agents, with the full support of Richard's Estate, submitted the manuscript for *Starlight* to McClelland & Stewart in July 2017, it felt as though we had received a final gift from this much-loved writer.

The manuscript was lightly edited. Grammatical errors, word repetitions, inconsistencies, and continuity issues were addressed, and occasional cuts were made for pacing, clarity, or flow. Punctuation was also added to aid reading, though only after close examination of the style used in *Medicine Walk*.

Given the incompleteness of *Starlight*, we wanted to let Richard close the larger narrative circle himself. On the following pages, we have included an essay by Richard titled "Finding Father," which was a finalist for the CBC Non-fiction Prize in 2015, and is previously unpublished in book form. Readers of *Starlight* will recognize the ways in which the themes and images in this deeply personal essay resonate beautifully with those in the novel.

Throughout the process of readying *Starlight* for publication, we were guided by something that Richard wrote:

"I once saw a ceramic heart, fractured but made beautiful again by an artist filling its cracks with gold. The artist offering a celebration of imperfection, of the flawed rendered magnificent by its reclamation. I loved that symbol until I came to understand that it's not about the filling so much as it's about being brave enough to enter the cracks in my life so that my gold becomes revealed. I am my celebration then. See, it's not in our imagined wholeness that we become art; it's in the celebration of our cracks . . ."

While it is a tragedy that Richard did not have the opportunity to complete this novel, what he achieved in *Starlight* is deserving of celebration. And what better tribute to Richard Wagamese, a man who believed in the healing power of story, than to share his majestic last novel with readers.

Finding Father

An essay by Richard Wagamese

IN THE DREAM I AM RUNNING. There's a dim trail through the trees making the footing dangerous. Everywhere there are humped and snaking roots of trees and rocks broad across the back as bread loaves and tall ferns and saplings that whip across my face. But I'm moving as fast as I can. The over-size gumboots I wear make speed even more treacherous. They slap and clap against my shins and flap around my feet at every stride. Still I run. There's a break in the trees and I can see the flash of white water from the rapids and I can hear the river's churning. From behind me I hear my pursuer. Heavy footfalls. Ravaged breath. I run hunched over, trying to keep the gumboots on my feet, fleeing for the safety of the river.

When I burst clear of the trees the sudden flare of light blinds me. But I sprint out onto the long, flat white peninsula of granite that pokes out into the river above the rapids. There are canoes there. I hope to jump into one and push it out into the current and down the chute of the rapids. I never get that chance.

Giant hands sweep me up. I'm spun in a wild circle. Large, strong arms enfold me. All I see is a whirl of long black hair like a curtain descending around me, falling over me, removing me from the world, the scent of woodsmoke, bear grease, and tanned hide, then deep laughter and the feel of a large palm at the back of my head. I'm laughing too as the gumboots fall from my feet. The world becomes the heat of the sun on my back and the feel of a big, warm heart beating against my tiny chest.

That dream is all I ever knew of my father.

I am Ojibway. My people occupy the large northern reaches of Ontario. We are bush people, river people, hunters, trappers, and fishermen. I was born in a canvas army tent on a trap line. The first sounds I heard were an eagle's cry, the slap of a beaver's tail, the crackle of a fire and soft roll of Ojibway as my family talked and told stories around that fire. I was born to be one of them. But time and politics and history prevented that from happening.

I became one of the disappeared ones. I became one of the thousands of Aboriginal children across Canada swept up in the Sixties Scoop. This was an action by the government in conjunction with foster-care agencies to arbitrarily remove kids from their people. We were transplanted hundreds and thousands of miles away from our home territories. Some were even sent to different continents. We were routinely sold to outside foster-care agencies. I was one of those disenfranchised kids. I disappeared into non-Native care before I was even two. I didn't make it home until I was twenty-four. Most of us never did.

My father's name was Stanley Raven. There were a number of men who adopted the name and role of father in my life when I was disappeared. None of them affected permanence. None of them fit the parameters of my dream. Stanley Raven was my one and only father and he died in a fall from a railway bridge the

37

year before I made it home. There are few pictures of him. A bushman's life seldom includes photographs and all I learned of my father were stories my mother and elder sister told. He lives for me in the rough and tangle of the northern Ontario landscape. I hear his voice in the rush of rapids, in the pastoral stillness of a northern lake at sunset, in the rutting call of a moose and the haunting soliloquy of a lone wolf howling at a gibbous moon rising above the trees and ridges. Stanley Raven. In those four syllables lays a history I can never reclaim and a connection to this earth, to the territory of my people I can never fully forge— and in this my wound became geography.

The land itself haunted me. I couldn't walk the Winnipeg River without an all-consuming tide of loss washing over me, could never stand on that railway bridge without scanning the rocks and trees for the dim path that might lead me to the camp he had set in the bush beyond it, could never hunt without the idea of him guiding me, teaching me, assuring me, could never watch the moon rise there without a wild keening rising from the depths of me.

So I set out to find him in the early fall of 1983.

"Where was the camp where I was born?" I asked my sister Jane.

"I don't think I could even find it," she said. "But it's across the bay from Minaki. There's a long narrow cove with big birches at the end of it. It's somewhere back there." In a landscape of bush and rivers it was an inadequate description. "Who's taking you there?" she asked.

"Just me," I said. "Something I gotta do alone."

She looked at me searchingly. Then she nodded. "Picking up the trail," she said.

I nodded. She never asked me any questions after that. Instead, she helped me fill a backpack with things I would need for a couple days in the bush and arranged for a family friend to loan me a boat motor for the trip. When I pushed off from the dock she stood there and watched and waved until I disappeared around a bend in the river.

Our family name, Wagamese, means crooked water. It's in reference to the Winnipeg River. It refers specifically to my great-grandfather, who worked a trap line through sixty miles of bush that ran along that river. It's my family's territory and my legacy even though we were all removed from it by the fall of 1983. But setting out alone on that river felt right to me and trailing a hand over the gunwale of the boat I felt a connection to its tea-coloured depths. If history has a smell then the mineral scent of that river on my hand is mine. If time can be erased and geography can return us to the people we were born to be then the wash of that water across my face was my act of reclamation and redemption. All through that trip downriver, around the cascade of rapids, into the long, sleek, flat muscle of channels, around the hem of islands jinned with white pine and birch and thrusts of pink granite, I let it seep into me and found release in the sudden spray of heron from a tree, the sovereign stance of a moose knee-deep in shallows eating lily pads, and the dark punctuation of a bear against the loose paragraph of the hills.

It took hours to get to Minaki. Then I turned south and west into a broad bay and began searching its far shore for the inlet my sister described. I found it just as evening was beginning to fall. There was just enough time to set up camp and light a fire before the thick, dark blanket of night fell over everything. I sat up late. When the moon rose I walked to the shore and looked up at millions of stars. I stood in the presence of a deep and profound silence and did not feel the least bit lonely.

In the morning I found an old pit. I dragged a log over and sat on it. I had no idea if it marked the site I was looking for, had no idea if it was my father's hands that had built it. But in the dappled light of that small clearing I chose to believe he had. I chose to believe that he'd held me in that clearing, clasped me to his chest, and cried tears of welcome then raised me up to the universe and spoke my name to it, introduced me to both it and the land around me in the language of my people, gave me both blessing and purpose right there in that small clearing so many years before. I sat there for a long time until the shifting light told me it was time to go.

I found my father on that journey. Found him in the shards of rock around an old fire. Found him in the scent of a river, in the ragged spire of granite cliffs, in the depths of the bush, and in the image of a ragged white pine perched alone at the top of a cliff lurched leeward by persistent winds, standing alone against time and circumstance, proudly like a prodigal returned to the land that spawned him.

I still have the dream, only now we run together into the light.

About the Author

Richard Wagamese, an Ojibway from the Wabaseemoong First Nation in northwestern Ontario, was one of Canada's foremost writers. His acclaimed, bestselling novels included *Keeper'n Me*; *Indian Horse*, which was a Canada Reads finalist, winner of the inaugural Burt Award for First Nations, Métis and Inuit Literature, and made into a feature film; and *Medicine Walk*. He was also the author of acclaimed memoirs, including *For Joshua*; *One Native Life*; and *One Story, One Song*, which won the George Ryga Award for Social Awareness in Literature; as well as a collection of personal reflections, *Embers*, which received the Bill Duthie Booksellers' Choice Award. He won numerous awards and recognition for his writing, including the National Aboriginal Achievement Award for Media and Communications, the Canada Council for the Arts Molson Prize, the Canada Reads People's Choice Award, and the Writers' Trust of Canada's Matt Cohen Award. Wagamese died on March 10, 2017, in Kamloops, B.C.

A NOTE ABOUT THE TYPE

Starlight has been set in Sabon, an "old style" serif originally designed by Jan Tschichold in the 1960s.

The roman is based on types by Claude Garamond (c.1480–1561), primarily from a specimen printed by the German printer Konrad Berner. (Berner had married the widow of fellow printer Jacques Sabon, hence the face's name.)

ALSO AVAILABLE

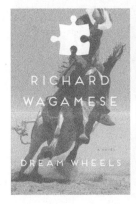

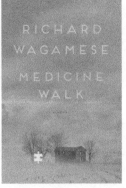